The Genehunter

SIMON KEWIN

STORM
CROW
BOOKS

The Genehunter was edited by Stephanie Lorée.

Jumpjacker originally appeared in Perihelion magazine.

22nd Century Genie originally appeared in Jupiter SF magazine.

ISBN: 978-1-9993395-0-0

For Pete, much missed

CONTENTS

1 - THE WRONG TOM JACKS

Simms stood in a circular white room, surrounded by the frozen heads of forty-two dead from the twentieth century.

He recorded every detail of the scene via his brain plug-in. Strictly speaking he had no business being here in the LA Bethesda Eternity Clinic and you never knew when information would come in useful. He didn't have the clinic's full client list, but each head sat encased within a two-meter silver cylinder, each bearing a small name plaque his plug-in could resolve. He stored each name away, the one he recognized and the forty-one he didn't.

"This way. The patient is over here."

The ratty, unkempt clinician he'd bribed crossed the room, glancing backwards at Simms to make sure he was following. Simms smiled at all of it. At the attendant, so proud of his ridiculous little world, at their insistence on the word *patient*, at the whole insane set-up. Did these people actually think *this* was eternal life? That they could conveniently bypass society's slide into hell? Be woken up in a golden future with all their cancers healed?

Elsewhere in the clinic there were full bodies preserved. The ones who could afford the deluxe package. *These* poor unfortunates had gone for the cheaper option. Simms almost felt sorry for them. He wondered what sacrifices each had made for even this.

He put it out of his mind. What did it matter? Wasn't any business of his. People with money paid and facilities like this met the demand. No harm in any of it. Perhaps it wasn't so different to what he did.

"This is him."

Simms stopped at the cylinder the attendant identified. It looked good. Tom Jacks, born 1954, *suspended* 2015. Yeah, right. Simms knew very little about him. A famous name, sure, but *this* Tom Jacks was a nobody. His searches had turned up nothing interesting at all. He was just a unique pattern of base-pairs that someone, somewhere was willing to pay for. Weird, sure, but he asked no questions. Collectors collected and he provided. He'd triple-checked they wanted *this* man and not his famous namesake. Most likely some relative researching the family-tree. Or it could be other things, but that was none of his business. Get the DNA, get paid, that was all that mattered.

The job made him uneasy, though. Damn thing was, he couldn't see why. It was straightforward enough. Maybe too straightforward. Things didn't go like this. It had only taken him a day and no one had threatened him, let alone tried to kill him. Here was the DNA, conveniently packaged up in a frozen brain. Somehow, he was sure, he was being played. He just couldn't see how.

He looked at the cylinder. The head was sealed inside, awaiting the dawn of the age of miracles. A dusting of frost coated the silver exterior. Was that right? Wasn't it supposed to be insulated?

"And you can extract a sample?" he said to the attendant. "You're sure it's clean, no decay?"

"Of course. There's an access point for biopsies. I'm sure you've heard the stories. How we don't really preserve anyone, just take their money to maintain empty chambers."

The attendant shook his head at the things people

believed. Simms said nothing. He wanted to get the job done and leave. Despite the cold and the sealed units, the place smelled of chemicals and decay. He was willing to bet the attendant came in here and talked to the damn heads when there was no one else around.

Simms took out the sterile needle he'd bought with him and handed it to the attendant.

"Here. I will test the sequence against his known phenotype. Anything less than 99% and the deal's off. Understand?"

Usually this was the time they started to bargain, see problems, remember expenses. The attendant merely assented with a nod of his head. Either he was a fool or he was playing a part. Simms watched as the man flipped open a small hatch in the side of the cylinder and inserted the needle into the dead brain within. A small screen lit up on the surface of the cylinder so they could see the needle's progress.

When he had the sample, Simms inserted it into the sequencer he carried. The device sampled the DNA, flashed through a simulated development cycle to full maturity, ran comparisons against the known historical details of this Tom Jacks. Within a minute, the results were communicated to Simms' brain.

His job would be a lot damn easier if everyone just got a number tattooed onto them at birth.

He looked at the attendant, waiting by the cylinder, breathing through his nose like this was the most exciting thing that had ever happened to him. Or like he might bolt at any moment. He could be a useful contact. This job was junk, sure, but you never knew what the next one would be. A cryogenic clinic attendant amenable to bribery might be a very useful person to know. Especially since Simms now had recorded proof he *had* been bribed.

"The sample is good. Here's your forty K."

Simms transferred the agreed sum, encrypted and untraceable. He saw the moment the money reached the attendant: the smile that brightened on the man's face was like the summer sun rising. Doubling your annual pay can do that. Which only troubled Simms all the more. The guy was an amateur. Someone was playing both of them. He'd been careful. He was always careful. When he crossed the line he made sure he left no evidence. Always gave clients the full speech about the uses to which recovered DNA could be put, word-for-word from the law. So far as the authorities knew, he accessed only public records. The bribe to this attendant was an infringement, sure, but no one would be able to prove a connection. He'd run through everything several times but could see no loopholes. It nagged at him. He hated that.

"I'd like to leave now," he said.

The attendant nodded as he sealed up the cylinder. They left Tom to his long wait and walked out, past room after room of frozen remains. Simms wished he could grab the names on all the units, but the doors were sealed. The attendant, whose name he still didn't know, was taking enough risk letting Simms do what he'd done. They could always come up with some line about visiting a relative if challenged, but if the clinic owners found out what their employee had done, it would be all over for him. For a set-up like this, public perception was everything.

They stopped at security doors while the attendant let the machinery sample his DNA. What was that all about? Controlling who came in made perfect sense, but controlling who left? Did they think the dead were going to rise up and try to escape? They'd seen too many old movies.

The security doors hinged open and they were back in the warmer air of the clinic's lobby, all polished marble and subtle music. Vases of flowers. *Real* flowers. A group of relatives sat in silence on the leather chairs, their expressions blank, no one talking. He thought about them all: the thousands and thousands of dead people in there, the thousands and thousands of estates paying fees in perpetuity. It was a beautiful thing. Maybe he should start one up himself. A few big contracts and he'd have enough money. Then he could sit back and enjoy life, let others do the work. He was willing to bet the myths about these places were true, often as not. Make it look good, professional like a real hospital, and people would pay. You didn't need to actually freeze the remains. Who would know?

Turning the pleasant fantasy over in his mind, he walked to the clinic's jump node. Normally he avoided them. The public jump infrastructure was shot to shit. But with a job came expenses and with expenses came the wonder of private networks. He instructed the system to take him back to London. He dialled in a few random jumps around the world *en route*, too, to throw anyone who might be following him. Private networks were more reliable, sure, but he didn't trust them to be any more secure.

✖

He knew something had gone wrong the moment he stepped out of the destination node. This was definitely not London Euston. Too clean, for one thing. Too quiet. He stood in a bare, square room; bright white walls, no doors or windows. The only way in or out was via the jump node he'd stepped from. He scanned it, as he habitually did, hoping to probe the network logs for anyone following him. The plug-ins required for this were highly illegal, but he happened to have a set hidden away in his skull. He got the node's address but nothing more. The gateway was deactivated. He checked his clock. Ten seconds had elapsed since he'd left the clinic. While you were in the jump network you technically didn't exist, had no consciousness of the passage of time. But, wherever he was, at least he had materialised. Everyone knew the stories about people trapped inside the jump networks, stuck for so long no one dared extract them to tell them. It was immortality of sorts, he supposed. Beat having your head cut off and frozen.

"Ah, Simms. There you are."

A disembodied voice from a metal grill in the opposite wall. He recognized it immediately. Things began to slot into place. So this was it? The whole job had been a GMA sting? Checking up licences?

"Agent Ballard of the Genetic Monitoring Agency," said Simms. "Hit another puzzle you can't solve? Having trouble telling the time, maybe?"

Ballard laughed his deep, rolling laugh. Was he nearby or somewhere remote? It didn't matter. It was typical of Ballard to lurk in the shadows. Simms really couldn't blame him. They'd met physically once or twice. If *his* face was as disfigured as Ballard's, if his features dripped like melted plastic, he'd stay hidden too. Acid thrown in his face, it was said, years back. Some thug resisting arrest. Ballard *could* have got it fixed long ago. Word was he liked his shocking appearance just fine. Found it useful when it came to playing the scary GMA agent.

"Simms, Simms. I'd really be more polite if I were you. I've pulled you out of the jump network to count how many laws you've broken today. Make my day any worse and I'll have to start looking *real* close."

The GMAn sounded delighted at the prospect.

"Investigate away. You won't find anything, but perhaps it'll make you feel like you're doing something useful with your life."

As he talked, Simms glanced around the room, trying to figure out an escape plan. He came up with precisely nothing. He had good plug-ins, unregistered military-grade tech that might be able to reactivate the jump mechanism. But they would take time to work and the GMA would have counter-measures. Plus, the less Ballard knew about his brain-boosters, the better.

"So," said Ballard. "According to the logs, you've been

commissioned to track down the DNA of a Tom Jacks. Purpose: addition to an unnamed collector's molecule library. All completely above-board and legal."

"That's correct. And well done on the reading. Some of those words are tricky."

"I'm puzzled, though," Ballard continued. "You specialise in musicians. Rock gods and dance divas from history. This man was a no one. Times hard are they?"

"I have to work to make a living. You should try it some time."

"Surely you're not intending to pass this Tom Jacks off as *the* Tom Jacks to some unfortunate citizen?"

"Obviously not. That would be illegal."

"Oh, but wait, what's this?" Ballard continued. "I see you're on your way home from the Bethesda Eternity Clinic, last resting place of Tom Jacks - the wrong Tom Jacks - currently cryogenically preserved and awaiting a cure for pancreatic cancer. Now that is odd, because the estate of *this* Mr. Jacks has granted no access to his remains."

"Which is why my trip was futile," said Simms. "Shame, but that's how it goes."

"So you didn't, say, illegally acquire this poor, dead man's DNA?"

"That's right. I didn't illegally acquire this poor, dead man's DNA."

"And the large sum of money you just sent from one of your accounts?"

Simms smiled, sure Ballard could at least see him. "A down payment on a slot at the clinic for myself. And thanks for being so concerned about my well-being."

Ballard snorted with laughter. "And if I let the techs loose on your brain and all those exotic plug-ins of yours, you're saying they won't find the DNA of Mr. Jacks encrypted away somewhere?"

A warrant for a full brain-dump on a suspect was still hard to get, even on a genehunter. They both knew that.

Simms had to hope it was too much trouble for Ballard to bother.

"Obviously not. That would also be illegal, Agent Ballard. I'm shocked at the suggestion."

"Or, I suppose I could visit the clinic myself," Ballard said. "Ask a few questions, see what really occurred?"

There was the weakness. The attendant should have expunged logs as instructed. He probably wouldn't stick to his story with Ballard bellowing away at him. Yet this was such a small-time job going to all that trouble made no sense. Ballard was having fun with him. Or… yes. He saw, then, what this really was. Some things didn't change.

"You could do all that, yes," said Simms. "And if I *have* accidentally transgressed some minor regulation, I suppose I'd have to pay some fine?"

"Approaching an official of a registered clinic without the estate's consent *is* a transgression, Simms."

"OK, Ballard. Just tell me how much you want."

"Forty K should cover it."

Simms considered for a moment. But there wasn't a damn thing he could do. If he refused he'd find his licence revoked one sunny day and that would be that. None of this *fine* would go near the authorities, sure, but he had no choice.

"Here's your money, Ballard. Now activate this node."

"My pleasure, Simms. And you be careful out there. There are all sorts of people trying to rip you off."

"Yeah. I heard that."

"Oh, and one more thing before you go. Who is *Boneyard?*"

Motherfucker. So this whole thing with the money was just a little extra for Ballard? He really, really hated the GMAn.

"Never heard of him. Friend of yours? Sounds unpleasant enough."

"A person I'd like to meet. I figure someone living in the gutter like you might have heard a whisper or two."

"And if I had?"

"Then you'd tell me. And we stay friends."

"Well, I'm sorry to be a disappointment."

"Oh, I'm used to it. But keep your ears open, OK, Simms? Bring me something useful and I'll think even more highly of you than I already do."

"Good bye, Ballard," said Simms. "And, just a suggestion, maybe spend that money you stole from me on cosmetic surgery? They can work miracles these days, you know."

✗

Simms stepped out of a node in the twelve-by-twelve array at Euston and pushed his way through the crowds out onto the streets. The stacktower where he lived was a twenty minute walk away. As he strode along, he sent a ping out to the agent who'd employed him on the Jacks job. He didn't know who his real employer was, of course. He knew the agent only as Mann. Which was not going to be his real name.

Mann replied immediately. Simms had the uncomfortable feeling Mann had known he'd be calling. Was Ballard mixed up in this somehow? Was Mann one of them, a GMAn? Was his name what passed for humour in the GMA? Christ. How was a guy to make an illegal living with these mosquitoes buzzing around, sucking his blood?

"Mr. Simms. You have the DNA sequence my client requested?"

The voice on the other end was calm, thoughtful. More the voice of a lawyer, someone used to weighing words carefully.

"I have it here," said Simms. "Plus documentation to prove provenance. Send payment and you can have the code right now."

"My client will have to test the DNA first, Mr. Simms. He or she does not intend to pay for some random sequence of numbers or the genetic sequence of, let us say, a dead baboon."

"You employed me because you could trust me."

"Still, I am under instruction. This is what we agreed."

"And if I send you the code and never hear from you again?"

"Then you would have cause to be angry and could lodge a complaint with the authorities."

"Yeah, yeah."

Simms sent the sequence off through the ether. They'd agreed encryption keys up front so there was no danger it could be intercepted as it traversed the net.

"Many thanks, Mrs. Simms. I shall be in touch at the earliest opportunity."

"Make sure you are. *Mann*."

Simms closed the link and turned his attention to the London street. The usual shit, piles of rubble, dead… things. The rain hammered down, a blur of spray on the hard ground. Why was it always raining? Surely it could be sunny occasionally? At least the rain helped wash the stench of decay and burning plastic away. He was old enough to remember how it had once been, when the streets were more-or-less safe and everything more-or-less worked. Now look at it. People used to say everything was going to hell. They didn't say it any more did they? They knew it had damn well *gone*.

He shook his head. Nothing he could do. He felt like this because he'd finished a job. Normally, some investigation would be bouncing around in his brain and he wouldn't notice his surroundings, the scowling people, the filth. Now he did. He hated the emptiness that inactivity brought.

Still, he had money to burn. Despite Ballard's cut, he'd be solvent once Mann's money came through. He could afford some downtime. He'd earned it. He called up an overlay from the relevant plug-in to shut London out. Immediately, an augmented version of the city replaced the ruined original. Trees lined spotless streets. The air smelt of roses. Contented people strolled by, hand-in-hand. Children played. They were dangerous, these false realities. People got lost in them. But he could control it. Right now it was fine.

XIX

Back home, he decided, what the hell, to ping Kelly. They hadn't spoken for, what, two months? She'd said she was going to get back to him. He was still waiting.

"Simms? What is it?"

To his surprise, the connection went straight through. She sounded harassed, though, like she didn't really want to speak to him.

"Just seeing how you are. You didn't call, I was worried."

"Yeah, right."

"Come on, Kelly. That's not fair. How many times do I need to apologize to you?"

"Oh, plenty more yet."

"OK, OK. Look, I wanted to know how you've been, for Christ's sake."

She paused for a moment before replying, like she was regretting her harsh words. So he liked to imagine.

"I'm fine. Busy. We're taking more in each day. We're going to have to expand to house everyone soon."

Another dig at him. He was to blame? He collected DNA. If other people used it to fill their private zoos with black-market copies of the great and famous, how was that down to him? He didn't operate the cloning vats, he didn't discard the damaged misshapes when they turned out wrong. He just did his job. Jesus Christ, everyone was on his back today.

"Look, Kelly, I'm sorry, OK? Sorry for what I do. Sorry for all the people who wash up there with you. It's not my fault, OK? None of it's my fault."

"Is that right, Simms?"

"Look, the thing is, work's been going well. I was thinking I could come over. I know the refuge always need funds. I could make a contribution. Something. I mean, no one likes to see the state these people are in. And maybe we could do something together. Go some place."

It was partly his age, but fleshbots didn't cut it for him. Even when they proxied for a real person somewhere distant. You still knew. You always knew. The thought of sex with Kelly, the real Kelly, would make everything - Ballard, London, Mann - *everything* better.

"You want to give us money from some DNA job? To help the people here?"

For a moment, he thought she was warming to the idea. "Yeah. I thought, you know, it would be something."

"You're unbelievable, Simms. Un-fucking-believable."

"Kelly, I…"

But she cut the connection. She was gone. He didn't try to ping her back.

His eyes focused on reality once more. He stood and stared out of his stackroom window at the grey clouds sweeping in across the London skyline. God *damn*. Why did he bother? It wasn't like she'd been completely innocent was it? Wasn't that what she was doing, out there in the Arizona desert? Making amends, trying to put something back? He got that. He'd do it himself, one day, if he could. Enough money from a few big deals and he could start his own refuge. They could run it together, the past forgotten. He could idle away his days in the sun while she divided her time between him and saving the world's cloning victims. All those brain-damaged Elvises and broken Mandela-copies living out their remaining years. She'd be full of gratitude. It would be beautiful.

Well. If he couldn't have her, a fleshbot would have to do. He'd paid for good emulation, although he could always tell when it - she - said or did something the real Kelly wouldn't. When its sex-toy programming was a little too near the surface. Weirdly, that was always an instant turn-off. But it would have to do.

And, if he couldn't have the real Kelly, he could at least have real acid. He didn't go in for direct-brain electronic analogues. He had the plug-ins, sure, but didn't use them. Nothing touched the real stuff. You could still buy it if you knew the right people. And Simms prided himself on always knowing the right people.

He made sure the stackroom was secure. The fleshbot booted up and moved towards him, swinging its hips a little too much to be believable. Sims sighed. He wondered what would happen if he gave *it* acid, too. That could be funny.

 ✕

The call interrupted him an hour later. It took him some time to grasp what it was. His com plug-in had trouble presenting his consciousness with an avatar of his caller. Had trouble *finding* his consciousness. Simms saw the sun turning into a vast face, becoming a mouth that screamed at him from the sky. Eventually he grasped someone was trying to reach him.

He shunned direct-brain drugs, but electronic detox could be damn useful. He kicked one off now, flushing the shit from his brain, sharpening the lines of reality around him. Slowly everything came into focus. Was his room always this small? Jesus. When he was ready he answered the ping.

"Hi, Mann. You got my money?"

"Can we talk?"

"What is there to talk about? I've done what you asked, now you pay the bill. That's how that works."

"I'd like to talk to you about another contract."

"Always happy to discuss a job. Let's complete the old one, then we can move onto the new one."

Didn't they have the money? But then, why bother to

get in touch? More likely, they had a problem with what he'd done. The wrong Tom Jacks after all? He couldn't see how, but he didn't need an unsatisfied customer seeking revenge. Especially some big shot used to getting their way. He wished he'd spent more time researching Mann, found out who he worked for. But the amount of money involved had been so small he hadn't bothered.

"Of course, of course. Here's your money, Mr. Simms."

The man's tone made it clear the amount was so trifling he'd simply forgotten to send it. Simms watched the zeroes counting up in his brain.

"OK," he said. "Now we can talk."

"Excellent. As a matter of fact, I'd like to meet up with you."

Alarm bells rang. He was still a bit out of it, a bit paranoid, but employers wanting to meet up generally meant bad things. He'd seen it happen often enough over the years.

"Why? This conversation is completely secure. No one can overhear."

"My employer is rather old-fashioned. He or she likes to, ah, *stare a man in the eye*. Apparently, by these means, he or she is able to judge character very effectively."

"You want to set up a meeting between me and your employer?"

"That's correct."

Mann had his attention now. Simms reached out and deactivated the fleshbot kneeling on the floor in front of him. What was going on here? It could all be a line. A convincing tale. Still, it could also be something sweet. A meeting with the money behind the façade generally meant they were taking you more seriously. Which meant more of the money. If they were unhappy with him, why go to all this trouble? They could deal with him from afar: a shot in the night, an EM pulse sending his plug-ins into meltdown. But not *polite conversation* for fuck's sake.

"OK," he said. "Tell me when and where."

✕

In the day he had spare, Simms took the time to do his job properly: find out who he was really dealing with, what their angle was. It didn't take a genius to work some of it out. The smoke and mirrors made it obvious. The party required DNA and they needed to be sure Simms was reliable. Now they knew. Problem was, Simms knew nothing about *them*. Knowledge was power. Anything could give him an edge, even if it only meant he could cut a better deal.

Standard trawls through the archives turned up nothing. Inevitably. With only a few hours to go before their meeting, unable to think of anything else, Simms decided to try Devi. Devi knew everyone.

Devi was another hunter, and hunters usually didn't mix. They were competitors. If you had a job another hunter knew something about they became your best friend. But if they decided to kill you and take the job themselves, they became your worst enemy. Devi had tried to kill Simms on at least three occasions.

Simms' ping went nowhere. Either she was offline or dead. He tried every ID he had but got a *no response* on all of them. OK. There were other ways to track down genehunters. None of them could stand to be unavailable for long in case a dream job came along, transporting them to a life of thrills and riches. Einstein's brain or the DNA of The Beatles. There was *always* a way to get in touch. You just had to know whom to ask.

He strode back to Euston, no overlays, still raining, and jumped half-way around the world to San Francisco. The Double Helix bar on Fisherman's Wharf was the closest thing genehunters had to home. It was an actual bar, a place people went to hang out, sit in shadowy corners, consume intoxicants and cut deals with each other. Like in the old days. Now such places were rare, old-fashioned, weird. For some reason, most hunters liked it. Perhaps for the same reason Simms preferred real acid. Nostalgia for the past, the good old days.

Inside it was quiet, the smoky air thick with murmuring. Glasses made of real glass clinked on tables that had once been living trees. People glanced up at him, looked away. He was known, welcome. Anyone could come into the Double Helix, sure, and sometimes tourists did wander in. But they left quickly, aware they weren't meant to be there.

Simms crossed to the bar. He felt relaxed. The Double Helix was, by common consent, neutral territory.

"What can I get you?"

Mac stood behind the old-fashioned bar, upturned bottles lined up behind him full of coloured liquids. Mac was always there, all wild hair and devil tattoos. His name wasn't really Mac. It just seemed like it should be, so everyone called him that. The joke was there were lots of Macs, clones taking turns to man the place. Day or night, there he was, never getting any older.

"The usual."

Most barmen would use a plug-in to work out what that meant. Facial recognition and a quick database lookup. Mac didn't need to bother with any of that.

"Quiet tonight," said Simms while Mac poured the Scotch.

Mac shrugged, unconcerned. Quiet was good. They all liked quiet.

"I'm after Devi," said Simms. "Heard from her?"

Mac looked into his eyes, assessing. He wouldn't want it *too* quiet. Bad for business to have his customers killing each other.

"Don't worry, just need her help," said Simms. "A few questions."

"This time."

"You know where she is?"

"I know where most of her is. The bits that are left."

"She's dead?"

"Oh no, she's alive. Amazing what they can do these days, huh?"

Details on Devi cost three more doubles, finest Scotch. Simms saw it as a win/win. Before he left he transferred more money, double what he'd already spent, then hit Mac with his final question.

"You heard of someone called Boneyard?"

Mac's eyes narrowed. He'd heard something.

"Sure."

"Who is it?"

"Don't know. Why you asking?"

"Because our old friend Ballard asked me, and I don't like to know less than a GMAn about anything. It's embarrassing."

Mac shrugged, like it was none of his problem. Which it probably wasn't.

"So, what?" said Simms. "What do you know?"

"That it's a thing, not a person."

"What else?"

"Only that it's something heavy. Bad for business."

"Ours or yours?"

"Same thing, ain't it, Simms?"

※

With the leads Mac had provided, Simms tracked Devi down to a hospital in Cairo where the medics were cultivating her a new set of internal organs. Seems her last job had gone badly wrong.

The roar of the great city hummed through the white walls. A thousand tubes and wires snaked from under Devi's covers to a silver box, where an array of lights blinked rhythmically. A box that more-or-less *was* Devi while her new body parts matured up from stem-cells. Devi looked deflated, her face more grey than olive. Her brown eyes were blurry and indistinct but she grinned her familiar, pained grin when Simms entered.

"How did you get in here?" she croaked.

"Told them I was a friend."

"Always were a convincing liar."

She shut her eyes, like she was drifting off to sleep already. He didn't have long to explain his situation. When he finished she nodded, as if everything made sense.

"What is it?" said Simms. "What do you know?"

"You got a voiceprint of this *Mann* of yours?"

"Sure."

Her plug-ins were fried so he had to relay the recording orally, letting his brain hardware control his mouth to make him sound like Mann. Wasn't perfect, but close enough. Sure felt weird, though.

"Yeah, that's him," she said.

"What do you know?" Simms asked in his own sweet voice once more.

"Remember Sanchez?"

"Sure."

"Your *Mann* was her *Smith*. She hooked up with them for some big deal about five years back."

"She's MIA, now. You're saying these people were responsible?"

It wasn't unknown for clients to dispense with their genehunters once they'd got the DNA they wanted. Dispense with them *permanently*. Cheaper than paying and it covered their tracks. The secret was to be indispensable. A rich client with a private zoo would always need more DNA. If they trusted you they would keep you on and everyone would be happy.

"No," Devi replied after a moment's thought. "I think you're good. Things went crazy for Sanchez after that. These people were straight. Kept quiet, paid their bills. You'll be OK as long as you don't fuck them around."

"Who, me?"

"Yes. You."

"She say anything else about them?"

"They're zookeepers, sure. A private menagerie of dead rock stars somewhere in the Caribbean. Word is they have more than that, too. A dark zoo of dictators and mass-murderers."

"And you're not telling me this to get me killed?"

"When *that* happens I want to be there."

Simms smiled, although Devi couldn't see it. "Thanks. You've been helpful. I owe you."

"Yeah."

Simms turned to leave. At the door he stopped.

"Oh, and Devi, get yourself fixed, OK? Shooting you in this state would be no fun at all."

She waved him away with a single finger.

"Mr. Simms."

"Mann."

Simms stood in an office, well-furnished but with no windows, no way of knowing where in the world he was. A room at the end of a jump address.

Mann looked like he sounded: a smart, highly-paid lawyer, dressed in expensive clothes, someone used to the finer things in life. He had no fear of Simms. On his own patch, protected by who-knew-what tech, he would be untouchable.

"So," said Simms. "Where's your master?"

"They may join us soon."

"Once you've checked me out."

"I'm sure they'll value my assessment of you."

"And, of course, they're watching everything that happens right now."

"No comment. But, if this situation is not to your liking, feel free to leave and we'll say no more about it. No harm, no foul."

"Sure, sure. Go on. The situation is to my liking. So

long as you can talk for them?"

"I have full executive authority in this regard."

"Yeah, like I said. So, what's the issue?"

"Tom Jacks."

"Tom Jacks."

"Tell me, did you think it odd you were employed to acquire the gene sequence of, how should I put it, the *wrong* Tom Jacks?"

That wasn't good. That wasn't good at all. Had they paid him just to lure him here? What was this, some twisted revenge set-up because the code wasn't to their liking?

"Now hang on. I established all that very clearly. The Jacks you wanted was most definitely not *the* Tom Jacks. What are you trying to pull here?"

"Mr. Simms, please. There is no need for anxiety. You completed the job we requested most capably and efficiently."

"Pleased to hear it."

"So, I'll ask you again. Did you think it odd?"

"It's not my place to question."

"Very well. Let me put it this way. If we had requested you retrieve the DNA sequence of the real Tom Jacks, the famous Tom Jacks, would your reaction have been any different?"

"I'd have wanted more money for one thing."

Mann smiled at that. "Understood. But, for the moment, recompense is not the issue here. The question is one of attitude. You have proved yourself a competent and discreet DNA Detective. I ask you again. If we *had* asked you to hunt the gene sequence of the real Tom Jacks, perhaps without anyone else knowing you were so employed, would you have been amenable?"

"*Are* you asking me to hunt the gene sequence of the real Tom Jacks? Or is this an interesting hypothetical conversation we're having?"

"That's what we're asking you, Mr. Simms."

The third voice came from behind him. Simms turned to see a woman stepping out of the jump node. He didn't know her voice although, when Simms turned to face her, a look of surprise flashed across her features. Something about his appearance had thrown her. Had they met once? He scanned her - face, plug-in aura - but got nothing. He also kicked off a jump network probe. Retrieving a source address could be useful. People tended to forget to cover things like that. While he waited for a response from the system he studied her. She was obviously rich. Super-rich. Everything about her made that clear. Not just the clothes and the jewellery. The rich could pick and choose metabolisms too, and this woman looked fabulous. Her eyes were old, wise, but she appeared to be no more than twenty.

The probe returned with her source address. It meant nothing to him, but he stored it away for possible later use and replied with a smile. "Then I'd take the job. Presuming we could agree terms and presuming you understood that retrieving the real Tom Jacks will be much, much harder. Perhaps impossible."

The woman crossed the room and sat down behind the desk. She seemed amused by something now as she looked at Simms. She nodded at Mann, instructing him to continue.

"We understand the difficulties you would face," said Mann. "For instance, there is the constant need to comply with the many and varied regulations governing the retrieval of deceased DNA sequences."

Simms had to stop himself from grinning. Rarely had someone asked him to break the law in such a polite way.

"We all have our burdens," said Simms. "But you learn how best to, ah, accommodate the law."

"Quite so."

It was Mann's turn to smile now. There was the briefest pause in the conversation. Mann and his employer communicating brain-to-brain.

"Mr. Simms, you recently spoke to an officer of the GMA. Can you tell us why?"

How had they known? Couldn't you at least trust government security agencies to be secure? Still, the question gave him hope. They were worried about him, worried *he* was GMA. Either that or they were very, very good actors.

Whichever, all he could do was tell them straight. "A corrupt agent called Ballard extorted money from me."

"Indeed?" said Mann. The lawyer studied him for a moment, forehead furrowing. Communicating again. They were debating him, assessing him. Damn shame he couldn't eavesdrop on them, but he didn't dare try.

"It must be difficult working with the GMA breathing down your neck all the time," said Mann. "Tell me, if we wanted you to work for us without them knowing you were so engaged, how would you feel?"

There it was. He should act horrified, walk out. But there were times you had to take a punt, trust your instincts. If you didn't, you stayed safe, legal - and poor. And he saw how clever they'd been. It hadn't been a test job. By registering a completely legal search for the *wrong* Tom Jacks they'd provided him the perfect cover in the hunt for the DNA they really wanted. No need to tell the GMA about the new arrangement. So far as they knew, the old job was still on the books. Simms had every right to pursue all possible means of acquiring *that* DNA, even if it meant excluding other individuals sharing, say, the same name. IDs got mixed up sometimes.

The woman and her advisor watched him intently. There was also the possibility he might not leave this room alive if he gave them the wrong answer.

"I'd feel cheerful about it," he said.

The rest of the meeting was detail. Some of the details were important: the money for one thing. The sum they agreed made it clear how serious they were. Anyone who could afford that much was not going to take being fucked around. At all. As they negotiated, Simms had to rely on plug-in overrides to keep himself from grinning like a child. This was good. Very good. Presuming he could find Tom Jacks - the real Tom Jacks - and presuming he could do so without the authorities knowing a damn thing, then he was set up. Some of those retirement schemes could finally become reality.

He felt only a single moment of doubt: a small voice in his head reminding him what they would use the DNA for. That sort of money definitely meant private zoos: illegal cloning and a life of slavery for an innocent individual who happened to share genetic sequences with a famous name. The voice had nothing to do with any plug-in. Simms pushed it out of his mind.

Once both parties had all the assurances and agreements they needed, Simms took his leave. He asked no questions beyond how to get in touch with them. He didn't bother with the statutory recounting of the terms of the law. They'd given him a month to find the rare and highly valued DNA of the dead rock star Tom Jacks. That was all he needed.

✖

He spent the next twelve hours trawling all the public and private networks he could think of, seeking out scraps of information that might prove useful. Reliable cloning technology had been developed early in the twenty-first century by the notorious Dr. Grendel. Interest in collecting the DNA of the rich and famous had taken off almost immediately. As a result, a lot of people had gone to a lot of trouble to hide or destroy tissue samples over the years. The more famous the individual, the more trouble. Which was why genehunters existed. Society may be shot to hell, but there were always the mega-rich who could afford anything and everything they wanted. Historical figures became one more commodity, the rarer the better. It wasn't unknown for a collector to destroy all copies of the sequence of some star of yesteryear to make their collection all the more valuable. Which made Simms' job tricky when it came to someone like Jacks. No doubt about it, that DNA was going to be very well guarded. If it even still existed.

Simms sat unmoving as terabytes of data streamed through his brain, AI search algorithms occasionally picking out an interesting detail, tagging and cross-referencing it with other hits. Hopefully his plug-ins would give him an edge. He fell into half-sleep as his brain worked, eyes open but not really seeing, an occasional snippet of interesting information bubbling up to his conscious mind. He was only distantly aware of growing thirst and hunger. He would stop soon, eat and sleep. This was how he always was when he had a new job. Single-minded. Other plug-ins kicked in to boost his brain and body, keeping him awake and alert as he searched.

At the end of it, he reviewed what he'd found. It wasn't much. He had plenty of people offering to sell Tom Jacks hair follicles, Tom Jacks blood, Tom Jacks semen. Simms dismissed them all. None offered any provenance and none were expensive enough to be real.

One story he did keep returning to: the famous Montreux concert that degenerated into a mass brawl, the death of three fans and the hospitalisation of thirty others. This was early in Jacks' career, when he'd fronted the extreme metal band *Teratoma*. Their gigs were always abrasive, confrontational. When, for an encore, Jacks appeared in front of forty thousand amped-up, screaming metalheads carrying an *acoustic* guitar and started to croon love songs, there'd been a riot. Fans invaded the stage. That Jacks was injured in the melee was beyond doubt. Shaky video footage showed him with blood all over his face.

More interesting were unconfirmed stories of his two lost teeth, punched out by an angry fan. The records showed he had orthodontic surgery two weeks later, but there were no details of the procedure carried out. There were no surviving images of Jacks in those two weeks that might confirm the story. But there were persistent stories of the teeth being retrieved and sold by fans before, finally, being acquired by a modern-day genehunter on behalf of an unknown client.

Simms could find no hard evidence to back up any of it. Most likely it was all urban myth. The hospital records from Jacks' operation were gone. The records of those injured in the riot did still exist. Nearly a hundred people had been treated at Montreux Riviera Hospital for broken bones, facial injuries, contusions. There was a good chance diagnostic samples survived from all of them. But they were of no interest. The name Tom Jacks wasn't anywhere on the list, and the musician would surely have been recognized if he'd been taken there.

On the other hand, there were numerous rumours of Jacks clones being sighted over the years, the by-now dead rock star spotted in the unlikeliest of places. Jump nodes, shopping malls, ball-games. Again, the stories were probably junk; the standard fare of brain-addled fans. But one detail had caught the attention of Simms' AI routines. Loosely corroborated by cross-references with both medical and travel records, he had two accounts of a supposed Jacks copy being admitted to a refuge for the victims of botched clonings. Supposedly a clone from DNA from one of the lost teeth. This was only fifteen years earlier, meaning there was a good chance the man still lived.

It was a weak lead, one he wouldn't have bothered with normally. But for this case, any trail was worth following.

That was the good news. The bad news was the refuge concerned. He obviously recognized the Arizona location. It looked like he'd be talking to Kelly sooner than he'd imagined.

⋈

To his surprise, the node key she'd given him twelve months earlier still worked. Had she left it active on purpose, hoping he'd arrive? Or forgotten to cancel it?

He materialised in the public reception hall. The room was cool, air-conditioned against the fierce Arizona heat. Another disembodied voice spoke to him, this one a little more friendly.

"Please state the purpose of your visit."

They had to be careful, of course. In the early days, refuges had been plagued with tourists and autograph hunters harassing the patients. Part of the reason they were stuck in the middle of nowhere. Simms explained who he was, who he'd come to see. A uniformed guard arrived to escort him through the clashing desert heat to another low building where he could talk to Kelly. He didn't get to see any of the patients. They were allowed to wander freely, leave if they wanted, but were kept well away from public eyes. Simms could see lines of white houses in the shimmering distance. A little oasis of trees off in the other direction. He wondered if Tom Jacks, his ticket to riches, was somewhere among them.

Kelly sat in a plain, square room, polished terra cotta floor tiles and whitewashed walls. She was the same willowy, black-haired beauty he'd known, but she looked taut, too, her features drawn into lines. Her eyes were red like she hadn't been sleeping well. Crying herself to sleep over him maybe. Yeah, right. He remembered the fierce, eager strength of her embrace. Now they managed merely to greet each other politely. They'd been both lovers and partners once, back in the day. There had been jobs neither was proud of. She'd quit hunting, gone to the light side and joined clONE. He'd promised to join her, but hadn't. That was all.

"What is it, Simms? I'm busy."

"The jump key you sent me still worked."

She shrugged, swept her hair out of her eyes. "Don't read anything into it. I forgot to cancel it. You're not welcome here. Didn't we talk about this?"

"I'd like to make that contribution we discussed."

"You discussed it. I refused."

"So your finances are so good you can afford the moral high ground?"

She shrugged, said nothing.

"Look," said Simms. "I understand your reservations. But no one's untainted are they? I can provide funds and you can do good with them. How is it helping your patients to refuse?"

She scowled, looked at him. Did she see through him? But it wasn't just an act. He meant it. He'd seen too many cloning disasters over the years. He wasn't a bad person.

"How much are you hoping to contribute?" she asked.

"You could do a lot of good with forty K, I expect?" He hadn't really thought about the amount. Forty seemed to keep coming up.

"We could do some good, sure."

"I'll transfer it to you now."

She shrugged, sent account details across without looking at him.

"This doesn't buy you anything, you know," she said. "It doesn't get you access to any DNA. Or to me."

"No, no. I know."

He'd hoped to spend time with her, imagined the two of them walking through the refuge. Maybe even bumping into the Tom Jacks clone, grabbing a DNA sample without anyone knowing. This wasn't going to happen. They weren't going to let him get close. Still, if he could somehow confirm Jacks was here, it would be something.

"I thought I could maybe sponsor an individual patient," he said. "You know, make a real difference to one person."

She was immediately suspicious, eyes narrowed. "What we do with the money is our business."

While she talked he sent out probes to her plug-ins. She had the usual array of brain add-ons. He'd once known some of her private keys. He hoped she'd forgotten to change those, too.

"I'm not asking to meet any patients, or even see them. I thought I could choose a particular individual to help. If you had a list, I mean."

It was an old technique, surprisingly effective. The suggestion of *a list* prompted one of her plug-ins to react automatically, pulling relevant names out of a database. Real names and their associated clone-twin names. As he'd hoped. She suppressed the data immediately, but not before he caught a glimpse.

He kept his expression blank but it didn't help.

"What did you do?" she said, standing up, sending her chair tumbling to the floor behind her.

"What do you mean?"

"You were in my head. What did you do? What did you see?"

"Nothing, Kelly. I…"

"That's why you came here, isn't it? Not to help them. Not to see me. You're working. Dear God, Simms, I don't believe you. How do you manage to fuck everything up so badly every time?"

"But…"

He didn't have time to say any more. Four guards burst into the room, weaponry aimed at him.

"Hey, OK, I just wanted to help is all," he said.

Kelly backed away from him. "You wanted to help yourself, you mean. Like always. You disgust me, Simms. Take your money and get out of here. And don't come back. I've deleted all your access keys."

"Kelly, please. I did want to see you, really."

But she turned and strode away. The security guards pulled him to his feet and prodded him out the other way, back to the jump node. He thought about fighting back. He might be able to stun them if he unleashed his offensive brain hardware.

He restrained himself. He didn't need to. Because the beautiful fact was that *Tom Jacks* was there on her list, along with the name of the clone who carried his DNA. *Luis Jesus*. And *that* was a name he had come across before. Come across very recently.

He still had a shot. He didn't need to break into the refuge after all. Life was good. He let the four grunts escort him to the jump node, a smile on his face.

XX

Simms stood outside the shining glass building. Another day, another hospital to break into. Except this was a real one, with real live dying people inside. Which all meant real security, too. Going to be a damn sight harder to infiltrate than Bethesda.

He'd worked on the place for over three weeks, more and more desperate. He'd tried hacking them, tried profiling key staff members to see if anyone needed urgent money. Nothing. He'd even engineered an injury – a self-administered cut to his leg – so he could get inside and take a look around. All he'd learned was the place was a damn fortress, private security keeping everything locked down. He'd discovered old tissue samples were kept on a sub-basement level, but that was it. All that efficiency meant there was a good chance the blood sample of Luis Jesus, one of those injured in the Montreux concert riot, would still be down there. The problem was getting to it.

He wondered if Kelly's clone knew his name was one of Tom Jack's pseudonyms. Jacks must have made it up that night, hoping to avoid attention. Most likely, the name was a joke on the part of whoever had created Jesus from that broken tooth years later.

It didn't matter to Simms. He had to get down into the basement, grab a sample and get out. And he had to do it now. Mann's month had all-but run out. All Simms' other schemes had come to nothing. Sometimes you had to dispense with subtlety and go in all guns blazing. Or at least, sneak in and *come out* all guns blazing. He didn't like the odds, but he refused to let this job slip through his fingers. Chances like it only came along once or twice in a lifetime.

His plug-ins got him through the door from the hospital's public area to the *Staff Only* corridors. He'd cloned the ID of one of the surgeons, a Dr. Echt, away speaking at a conference in the Far East. Simms had gambled the hospital systems wouldn't be paranoid enough to cancel Echt's access for the week he'd be away. It looked like the gamble had paid off. Simms walked down the deserted corridor, feet clacking on the hard floor. He resisted the temptation to tread softly. The key to deals like this was to look like you belonged. Ask questions rather than answer them.

Two women approached him down the corridor. He'd profiled everyone he could find at the hospital. They were admin, high up, but in a different department to Echt. He ignored them, like he was deep in thought. People at work didn't smile at each other. The women passed by, paying him no attention.

The hospital was big, rambling, but he had the floor plans stored in his brain. He made his way to the lift that descended to the basements. Instead of using it, he pushed open the door to the adjacent fire stairs. There were cameras everywhere and a lift could become a cage at the touch of a button. Stairs at least gave him a shot.

Two levels down he reached another set of security doors. Echt had no access down here, so Simms resorted to hacking. He unleashed the electronic wizardry in his cranium. If someone asked what he was doing, his only plan was to start shooting. But this was a storage level; he'd calculated few people would come down here. And most likely they'd take the lift. Another reason to use the stairs.

After a solid minute of work, the locks on the basement door succumbed. Electronic systems were easy to fool given the right tech. What you couldn't do was stop all the background logging and cross-checking. He knew he wouldn't have long before they came for him.

He flicked on the lights. No point hiding now; it was all about speed. He'd hacked the tissue catalogue and knew precisely which cabinet and which drawer he needed. He ran, muscles and brain amped up to the maximum. It was cold down here, refrigerated, but he barely noticed. It took him only twenty seconds to locate the sample of Luis Jesus. Five less than planned. Perhaps he had a shot at this after all.

The blood sample was old, dried to a dull brown. They kept them for a hundred and one years in case of legal challenge. Sometimes he loved the forces of law and order. He might not get good DNA but it was a chance. He sampled the blood, storing the sequence for later analysis.

The first blaster shot caught him in the shoulder, spinning him round. Lucky, really: it meant the next shot missed *and* he was facing the right way to see the two security guards standing by the door to the stairs. His med plug-in began saturating his system with painkilling drugs as he assessed the situation.

"On the ground. Now!" the guards called. They sounded cross. Simms looked like he was going to comply, moving slowly. Then, muscles acting at reflex-speed, he pulled out his blaster and fired. Resorting to shooting was an act of desperation, an admission of failure. He'd run out of other options. Guided by his military-grade aiming software, his two shots found their targets. The guards sagged to the ground. They'd wake up in a couple of hours. He wasn't being humane. If the authorities *did* catch him, a couple of murder charges would just make everything worse.

He ran. The police would arrive soon, and his defences would be nowhere near as effective against them. His plan was this: run like hell for the doors before they got to him. It wasn't his best plan ever, he had to admit.

He raced up the stairs three at a time and into the corridor. He heard running feet as more guards converged on him. Sirens and bells in the distance. Time for his exit strategy. There were two other doors to the hospital, including one to admit deliveries too big for the hospital's jump nodes. That door might not be locked down. The danger was they'd work out he was using Echt's ID and track him through the building. Or they could follow the trail of blood he was leaving on the floor...

Ninety seconds later he made it to the cargo door. It stood half open, easy for him to duck through. Metal crates had been neatly stacked just inside and he could hear the motors of some sort of transport vehicle presumably delivering more. He hadn't spotted any more security. Maybe they'd all gone to defend the jump nodes like he'd hoped. He was shaking, either with excitement or loss of blood, but he ignored it. He darted for the door, dropping the Echt ID from his brain and adopting another, unrelated one prepared for the purpose.

The second shot slammed into him before he heard it. The ground threw itself up at him and he knew no more.

"So, Simms. Here we are again."

Simms came round in another small, square room, somewhere still in the hospital judging by the medical paraphernalia around the walls: the oxygen feeds and alarm buttons. Everything was spotless, sterile. He lay on the hard floor. They could at least have found him a bed. Still, he was alive. Armed GMA agents guarded the door. Someone leaned over him. No mistaking that face.

"Agent Ballard."

"You're under arrest for the illegal acquisition of the DNA of Tom Jacks. Plus the contravention of numerous other laws I haven't even thought of yet."

Simms tried to think straight through the veils of pain filling his brain. How much did Ballard know? His GMA plug-ins were secure from Simms' intrusions and his ruined face was, as ever, impossible to read. How much did he really understand about what was going on here?

"I'm sorry, don't have any such DNA."

"Really, Simms. Is that the best you can do?"

Simms rose to his knees, tried to stand. He'd feel better if he could look Ballard in the eye.

"It's the truth."

"So you're here visiting a dying relative, is that it?"

Simms calculated for a moment, trying to find a way out. It was hard when people insisted on keeping secrets. In the end, he decided to adopt the simplest approach.

"OK, Ballard, I *have* just illegally acquired a DNA sample. But I assure you it isn't Tom Jacks."

"Who then?"

"One *Luis Jesus*. Check the records if you like. He has no connection to Tom Jacks."

There was a slim chance Ballard knew Jacks and Jesus were one and the same. Simms figured it was a risk worth taking. He watched Ballard's eyes, the brief moment of vacancy while he checked on the name.

"Never heard of him."

"No reason why you should. He's a nobody."

"Then why go to such lengths? You could have been killed. You still might be."

Was this further extortion? Pay a fine and go on his way? He doubted it. Ballard was corrupt, sure, and a bully. But he did his job. Unless a bigger prize was dangled before him. Simms decided to gamble.

"You want the truth? I heard a rumour about him. In connection with *Boneyard*."

Ballard's eyes narrowed. Simms had his attention. Whatever Boneyard was - and Simms had absolutely no idea - it was of great interest to Ballard.

"What connection? And why are you looking?"

"Because you asked me to."

"Don't get smart with me, Simms."

"I'm serious. Boneyard is of interest to you. And that means I'm in a position of power if I find out about it."

"It?"

"Uh-huh. Boneyard isn't a person. It's a thing."

"What sort of *thing?*"

"Haven't got that far yet."

"And you think you can bribe me if you find out?"

"I think I can bargain with you if some other minor contravention of the law comes to your attention."

Ballard studied him for a moment. This could go either way. The GMAn could arrest Simms and charge him, tie him up long enough to blow all hope of completing the Jacks job. Or he could believe Simms' line. It all depended how much Ballard wanted this Boneyard. Simms' chances hung by that thread.

"Tell me the connection," said Ballard.

"Not until I have something concrete. I'm acting on a whisper here and it may come to nothing."

"Tell me who the whisperer is."

"Sorry, can't reveal my sources. Look, Ballard, you can drag me off to some dungeon and ream the facts out of my brain, but what good will that do you? This Boneyard is well-hidden. I know next to nothing. But if I'm allowed to operate, maybe I can come up with something for you. I don't need you as an enemy."

"And you think all this can be made to go away?" Ballard indicated the hospital with a wave of his hand. "All the crimes you've committed today?"

"I think *you* can make it go away. Come on, we both know this little scene is nothing. Unimportant. It's beneath you, Ballard."

Ballard took a step forward. Simms braced himself for a blow. Instead, Ballard jabbed his finger into Simms' wounded shoulder. A moment of raw agony cut through him before his med plug-in could react.

"OK, Simms," Ballard said, whispering into his ear. "Here's what's going to happen. I'll let you *operate*. For now. Bring me Boneyard and we can remain friends. But I'll be watching, Fuck with me and I'll know about it."

Make them think they'd won when they'd lost. It was the only way.

"Whatever you say. Now, can I go? I have work to do. Real work."

Ballard stepped back and pulled open the door. "Get out of here. And take my advice, Simms. Leave Montreux before the local police get to you. They won't be as friendly as me."

"Just what I was planning to do."

"Mann?"

"Mr. Simms. You certainly like to leave things until the last minute."

"I have what you want."

"Excellent. Send it over for assessment and, assuming all is well, we'll complete the transaction as agreed."

"It's on its way now."

Now this was Simms' idea of a hospital. A tropical beach to convalesce on. His own nurses on hand to bring him everything he might need. No one trying to kill him. Bliss.

He yawned, stretched, enjoying the warmth of the sun on his face. He sipped his mojito. He was beginning to like them almost as much as Scotch. No doubt about it, the money from the Jacks job was making him a very happy man.

Except. Problem was, he was already getting bored. He could feel that itch. What was going on in the world? Who was in the Double Helix right now, cutting a deal? Above all, what the hell was he supposed to *do*? He'd thought to take a year, two years off. Get fixed. Chill out. Two weeks in and he was already wondering if Mann was trying to reach him with another name.

He decided to make a few calls. Where was the harm in that? He put himself back on the net and pinged Devi, partly to see if she'd made it through her procedure, partly to send the fee for her help. Always good to keep contacts sweet. Devi accepted the money with something like her usual abrasiveness. When Simms sent her the view from *his* hospital window, she cut the connection, swearing creatively.

Simms then transferred 100K to the account Kelly had given him back in the refuge. Anonymously. Perhaps she'd realise it was from him and perhaps she wouldn't. That was up to her. But he found the act gave him a strange sensation, made him feel better about things.

He was about to vanish from the net again and ask for another mojito when the ping came through from Ballard.

"So, Simms. How is the investigation going?"

For a moment, Simms was confused. Surely Ballard would know the Jacks job was over by now?

"Investigation?"

"Don't play games with me. You know what I mean. Our agreement over Boneyard."

"I wouldn't call it an agreement. More of an… *understanding*."

"Is that right? Well, just as long as you *understand* I own you now, Simms. I've got enough evidence to put you away for about three centuries. But if you're useful to me I might forget about it."

Simms thought about cutting the connection there and then. Easy enough to hide away, switch IDs, kill off Simms and become someone else. He had the money to do it, now. Problem was, he *liked* genehunting. And if he wasn't Simms any more he'd be back to square one, an untrusted unknown, one among thousands.

"OK, Ballard," he replied. "I think I can get my head round what you're saying. But I'll work at my pace, in my own way. Have you got that?"

"What I've got, Simms, is your licence in my hands. And if I think you're being unhelpful to an agent of the GMA then I'm going to have to sit down and review it."

"Yeah, yeah. Look, I'll be in touch. Sweet of you to call, and I'm sure you've missed me, but there's really no need. I'll bring you something when I have it."

"Make sure you do."

Simms did cut the connection, then. He called for the mojito and sipped at it, lost in thought, watching the sun melt into the sparkling blue sea.

So. What the hell was this *Boneyard* anyway?

2 – THE ZOMBIES OF DEATH

The ping roused Simms from confused nightmares. He lay slumped on the couch of his London stackroom, neck ricked at a painful angle. He sat up blearily. Very few people knew the private address the message had come in on. But Mac, the barman over at the Double Helix, was one. Too useful a contact to exclude. Still, Simms had to be careful. You never knew for sure what you were dealing with. You couldn't just trust people these days.

"Yeah?"

"Simms. Someone trying to reach you."

"Someone I know?"

"Someone you know."

The agreed code phrase. No one pointing a blaster at Mac's head. Simms sat up, interested. His first call since the Tom Jacks job. It was about time. Waiting around was the worst part of being a genehunter. Despite the wonderful opportunities for hedonistic excess all that money gave him, he was bored.

"Go on."

"Collector called Lund. Came in here looking for you, says you've worked for him before."

Simms checked the ID Mac sent along with his

message. The real Lund, for sure. An actual, legitimate molecule collector. Most of Simms' clients used the story as a cover for their private zoos of illegal clones, of course. With Lund, it was the truth. Weird, but there it was. The guy was harmless, reliable and rich. Simms' favourite kind of person.

"OK. Is he still there?"

"He left a jump key, good for twelve hours."

"Thanks, Mac. I owe you."

"Forget it. After your Tom Jacks bash I still owe you."

Mac cut the connection. Simms sat back, looking around, trying to work some movement into his neck. His room was a disgrace. It was like wild animals foraged there while he was away. His fleshbot lay on its back, limbs splayed at an awkward angle, head turned as if watching him. Damn thing was always crashing these days. Time he replaced it.

He needed coffee. As with all intoxicants, he preferred the real thing to any direct-brain analogue. He slouched into his kitchen to load up his expensive, antique espresso coffee maker with expensive Jamaican Blue Mountain.

A new job. OK. That was good. He'd been drifting too long, wondering what to damn well *do*. He began to make plans. He'd jump over to Lund in Newer York right after the caffeine had kicked in and he'd gotten himself cleaned up. The coffee machine began to steam and rumble. It was going to be a good day after all.

So he thought, right up to the moment he heard the knock on his door.

Alarm cut through Simms at the sound. No one ever knocked on his door. Who knocked on doors any more? A whole array of alarms should have gone off before anyone got close.

No one knew he lived there. OK, there was one person, but Kelly wasn't going to turn up out of the blue. Perhaps he should have moved somewhere remote after all. Spent some of that money on a fortress. But this cramped London stackroom was safe because it was anonymous and unremarkable. He was one lonely citizen among millions. No one would ever come looking for him here.

Except now, someone had.

While he scrabbled around for a weapon he ran through all the people it could be. It was a depressingly long list. An unhappy client? Always a possibility. He prided himself on never cheating, of supplying genuine DNA or no DNA at all. Other hunters were less scrupulous. If they couldn't find the sequence they'd been charged to track down, they just handed over something close. Still, mistakes happened. He was only human. And there could always be relatives objecting to him copying and selling the gene sequences of a loved one. He got that.

Genetic Monitoring Agency? Perhaps Ballard or some other GMAn had come to scare him. Doing so every now and then seemed to be in their rule book. Another hunter? Unlikely. Even Devi, who knew everyone and everything, didn't know where Simms lived. Probably. Some clONE fanatic, come to gun him down for supposed crimes against the *regened* community? Maybe.

But he doubted it. He'd been careful. It *had* to be Kelly. She knew where he lived, had access keys to get through his security. She'd come to see him after all. Say sorry, maybe. Say something at least. Damn shame he was such a mess. He looked at his distorted face in the gleaming silver of the coffee machine. Christ. He could have shaved once in the past week, couldn't he? Maybe it was time he paid for a metabolism-mod plug-in to take care of shit like that.

While he tried to smooth his hair into something vaguely humanoid he interfaced with the room's security so he could get a view of her, standing there outside his door. The thought of seeing her made him feel weird. Happy.

But it wasn't her. Wasn't anyone he recognized. A man stood there: shortish, oldish, unremarkable. No weaponry or military brain hardware of any kind. He stood unmoving, bundled up in his grey coat, waiting patiently. His plug-ins identified him as Gideon Jones, an unremarkable citizen with no connection to Simms whatsoever. Had he just knocked on the wrong door?

Maybe, maybe not. Only one way to find out. It was turning into an interesting day after all. Simms readied the short-range blaster he'd unearthed, checked his security systems were primed, then spoke.

"Yeah?"

"Mr. Simms? May I come in and have a word?"

"Why?"

"My name is Gideon Jones. I've been sent here by Kelly. From the refuge in Arizona. May I come in?"

"Why?"

"I mean you no harm. I have a message for you."

Simms thought for a moment. Why would she be getting in touch with him? They'd parted on bad terms. Bad even by his standards. She'd made it pretty clear she wanted nothing more to do with him. But he was plagued by thoughts about her, wondering what she was doing or thinking. It was weird. But if this was a way to get back in touch with her, he'd take it.

He checked once again to ensure the man was alone and unarmed then instructed the room to let him in.

Gideon Jones stepped inside, closed the door quietly behind him, then unleashed an overwhelming EM attack on Simms' brain plug-ins. A storm of agony raged through Simms before he could react. He blacked out even as he slumped to the floor.

✕

When he came round, pain thrummed through his head and he couldn't move. Restraints bit into his wrists and ankles. There was something around his forehead, too, tight like a strip of elastic. He reached out with his plug-ins to interface with the stackroom. No response. From anything. All his brain hardware was offline. How was that even possible? He felt more vulnerable than he had for years. It was like losing his sight and hearing and all his other senses in one go.

"Ah, Mr. Simms. You're awake at last."

Gideon Jones - or whoever he was - stepped into view. He stood over Simms, still wearing his grey coat, still the dowdy, drab individual Simms had seen at the door. An unremarkable face like millions of others. Yet this man had effortlessly overcome Simms' very expensive defences.

Jones had his hands in his pockets. Simms expected him to pull a blaster. That was how it went in these situations. Instead, the man just stood there like he didn't know what to do next. He smiled a regretful smile.

"Who the hell are you?" Simms asked. "And how did you manage to spoof my defences?"

"That's the least of your problems just now."

The man appeared to come to a decision. He pulled something from his pocket. Not a blaster, a crucifix. A golden crucifix with a long, sharpened shaft, more like a dagger. That *definitely* hadn't shown up on the security scans. It told Simms everything he needed to know. *Forty Days*. He hadn't even included them in his list. He'd have preferred Ballard. He'd have preferred just about anyone.

"You're evil, Mr. Simms. Did you know that?"

The man knelt like he was going to pray. Instead he brought the viciously sharp crucifix towards Simms' face. Simms watched the tip. It was hard to look at anything else.

"Really?" said Simms. "That's weird because you're the one holding a piece of sharpened metal in my face."

The man shook his head.

"You are a genehunter but I am doing the Lord's work. And you should know that while *he* forgives any sin, I'm much more fallible."

It was pretty clear how this was going to go. Simms

didn't keep up to date, but he knew the church disapproved of cloning. If you created a human from DNA you created another immortal soul, right? Were you, therefore, God? Or, if not, that meant clones were soulless beings, forever excluded from heaven. Or was God somehow playing along, conveniently chipping in with new souls as needed?

It was a debate that kept hundreds of scholars and clerics tied up in knots. And it fuelled fundamentalists like Forty Days, whose response to the fascinating liturgical question was to go around wiping out clones and anyone involved in their creation.

Simms struggled against his restraints but managed only to pull a muscle in his side.

"The device around your head is suppressing your plug-ins," said Jones. "Still, I'd feel happier if they were properly disabled. This cross is sharp enough to puncture your skull. I can trepan the electronic demons from your head with it. Shall I do that? Don't worry, the brain can't feel pain. Once I'm through the skin and bone it won't be too bad."

Was this what they did? A fucking sermon before they killed you?

"What is it you want?"

The man ignored Simms' question. "Although it might be quicker and easier to go in through your eye-socket, follow the pathway of your optic nerve into your occipital lobe. Would you prefer that?"

The cross was so close to Simms' left eye its tip was blurred. Instinctively Simms checked his med plug-in was ready to flood him with painkillers. It, too, was offline.

"Hmm, Mr. Simms? What do you think?"

Simms wanted to flinch, pull his head to one side, but didn't dare move.

"I get a choice?"

"Oh, there's always a choice, isn't there? We are free souls, made in the image of the Lord. Or do you think, given your profession, we're all just biological machines, products of our genes?"

Weird how the Forty Days nuts ended up sounding like the clONE nuts, even though they despised each other.

"I don't think that."

"Is that so?"

"Look," said Simms. "This is fascinating I'm sure, but I'd prefer it if you just killed me now."

"Actually, I haven't come here to kill you."

"Really? Only, I did get the impression that was why you'd come."

"No. I've come to give you a message."

"From Kelly?"

"Obviously not. Even she doesn't hate you this much."

"And you couldn't just send me this message? You had to do all this first?"

"I wanted to be sure I had your attention."

"Well, let's assume you have my attention."

The man paused for a moment, then stood up. He brushed invisible dust from his coat with a gloved hand, then cleared a space on the couch and sat down. "You've been asking questions about *Boneyard*."

"And you know what that is, right?"

"I do."

"OK, so what is Boneyard? A thing? A place?"

"A place. Or it will be."

"What does that mean?"

"I'm not going to tell you that."

Why hadn't the stranger killed him? Why this game? It made no sense. "So… you're here because God told you to give me an annoying puzzle?"

"I'm here to give you some valuable information."

"And why would you do that?"

"To see what you do with it. You may run off to Agent Ballard with it and hope he'll look after you. You may choose to ignore it. You may try to find out more. Whatever you do, we will know and that will be of interest to us."

"Why?"

"I'm not going to tell you that."

"OK, so what, exactly, are you going to tell me?"

"I could tell you many things, Mr. Simms. I could tell you clONE has you on an active hit list. But you knew that. I could tell you Agent Ballard is tracking your every move, although, again, you probably guessed. I could tell you Kelly *hasn't* told you about Eloise. Your daughter. I could tell you Tom Jacks has now been illegally cloned and is currently an embryo of a few thousand cells. But I won't tell you any of those things. Instead, I am going to tell you something about Boneyard."

"What do you mean, *daughter*? What the hell are you talking about?"

"Hush, now. Best you just listen, eh?"

"But…"

"Please, Mr. Simms. I can make you quiet, you know."

"I'm listening."

"The Soldiers of Megiddo gather."

"Huh?"

"You heard me. That's my message."

"*The Soldiers of Megiddo gather.* What the fuck is that supposed to mean?"

"Please, Mr. Simms. There is no need for profanity."

"A knife in the eye is OK but swearing isn't?"

"It depends on whose eye."

"OK. *The Soldiers of Megiddo gather.* Do please tell me what that refers to, if you'd be so kind."

"That's up to you to discover, Mr. Simms. Should you choose. But we'll be watching to see what you do, have no fear."

"Who is *we* exactly?"

"So many questions, Mr. Simms. Now, I'm going to knock you out again. You'll awake in eight hours. All your plug-ins will be functional once more. I shall be long gone and you will have no means of locating me. Is that all understood?"

"Yes, but…"

The man held up his hand. "Enough. You'll be perfectly safe, I assure you. For now, at least."

He had no choice. Perhaps he should have stayed on that beach after all, enjoyed his retirement. Except, despite everything, despite the trembling racking his body, he was almost enjoying this. At least he knew he was alive.

"So how do I get back in touch with you?"

"You don't, Simms. We get in touch with you."

"But…"

Before he could reply, unable to resist in any way, Simms blacked out for a second time.

His head still throbbed with heavy pain when he came round, but Jones had spoken the truth. Simms lay on the floor of his stackroom, all his plug-ins miraculously functioning once more. He sat up, groaning, clutching his forehead, waiting for analgesia to kick in. He felt like he'd been beaten up and left for dead, not like he'd slept for eight hours straight. A stinging sensation prickled all across his back, as if he'd been lying on something sharp. He also had a sharp pain on the back of his head. Must have cracked his skull when he fell over.

Eight hours. Damn. Lund had only given him twelve to get over to Newer York. He didn't have much time left and he was in no state to visit a client. He had a lot to think about – a hell of a lot – but he didn't want to consider any of it just then. Lose himself in activity, that was the way. He climbed to his knees and stood up. He needed to clean himself up, eat and drink, go see Lund. Everything else would fall into place when the time was right. Probably.

"Mr. Simms. I was beginning to think you weren't coming."

"My apologies, Mr. Lund. I was delayed with another client. I'm sure you know how it is."

"Of course."

"It's been, what, a year?"

"Correct. Do come in and I'll let you know what I want."

Lund lived in the sky above Newer York. He'd positioned his cloudhouse directly over the slums that stretched along the east bank of the Hudson. People like him did that. Liked to hover half a mile up in the air to take in the sights and sounds of misery and brutality down there on the ground. Probably threw parties to watch when things really kicked off. Simms didn't comment. What was the point of being rich if you couldn't remind yourself what it was like to be poor? Maybe he should find something similar for himself. Then a visitor like Gideon Jones couldn't come knocking on his door.

Inside, Simms and Lund exchanged the usual pleasantries for a few minutes. Tedious, but you had to do it. They stood in an observation room: glass walled, glass floored, telescopes set up for gazing down on the slums. Simms could see fires down there, vertical lines of smoke between all the shacks, humanity reverting to the stone-age. He could see people crawling around too, but couldn't tell what they were doing.

"My collection is this way," Lund said finally, leading Simms through echoing rooms into his inner sanctum. They walked into a series of large, adjoining halls out of sight of any window. It was like an art gallery, with framed portraits adorning the walls. Pictures of the famous people in his collection. Except that beneath each, encased in a small crystal cylinder, was the DNA of the subject itself.

It had been an impressive collection of twentieth and twenty-first century musicians when Simms had last been here. Now it was amazing. Lund had *everyone*. Simms would have given almost anything for an hour alone in there with a DNA sequencer. But he wasn't going to get it, of course. People like Lund guarded their collection fanatically. Rarity was part of the appeal, owning the DNA your rich friend didn't. For some, DNA collecting was just an investment. A rare commodity that was therefore valuable. For people like Lund that wasn't it. They were just big kids trying to outdo their friends.

Whatever. Their motives were no concern of Simms.

They stopped at an empty frame in the wall. No portrait, no crystal slug. Lund didn't have everyone after all.

"This space is for *The Zombies of Death*," said Lund. "You know them?"

Simms didn't, but searched for them and replied without pause. It was all about looking like you knew what you were doing. "Of course. Early punk four-piece from London. Obscure; played together three years, then split up. Often cited as influential."

"Can you get them?" asked Lund. His eyes glowed with anticipation. What did people like him do when they finally got all the DNA they wanted? Maybe that was when they moved into cloning and zoos.

Simms paused, looking like he was weighing up odds, calculating risks. He could get them, he was sure. He had a pretty good idea where to find two of them already. The singer and lead guitarist, inevitably. Devi had harvested them a few years back and she would certainly have kept a copy for herself. There was nothing sweeter than a client paying you for a subject you already owned. In a way, genehunters were collectors, too. Only they did it for sound, sensible reasons. Money.

"I think so. Do you have a time scale?"

"No. But you should know I've employed another investigator to track down the band. The first one to get back to me gets two million. The second one gets nothing.

That's the deal."

"You going to tell me who the other is?"

"No."

Simms considered. He had no leads on the other two members of the band: the poor, forgotten bassist and drummer. Still, they'd been part of a thriving scene. Chances were each had gone on to gig with a bunch of other groups. His initial scan could find no reference to any early deaths, so often the problem with musicians.

"Very well, Mr. Lund. I believe I can track down the DNA you require. Of course it will take a little time to make absolutely sure the code is 100% pure, but I know you expect nothing less."

"Of course." Lund sent over a ping address to Simms' brain. "When you're ready, you can reach me on this."

They shook hands and left Lund's collection of singers and rock-stars to their long, silent wait. At Lund's private jump node, Simms hesitated before giving the system his destination. He thought about returning home, crashing out. He'd managed to hide it from Lund but he felt like death. What the hell had Gideon Jones done to him? On second thoughts, though, he dialled in the address of the Double Helix and jumped across the continent for San Francisco. What he really needed was a drink. By which he meant *several*.

※

Simms placed his fifth shot of whisky on the table in a shadowy corner of the bar. He was no nearer to deciding what to do. Too much buzzing around in his brain. Gideon Jones. Boneyard. The GMA, clONE. Eloise, for Christ's sake. Now Lund and the Zombies of Death gig. As soon as he tried to focus on one thing, the others nagged away at him for attention.

OK. One problem at a time. Gideon Jones and Forty Days. What was all that about? He'd found their message soon enough, glimpsed it in the mirror while undressing for his shower. Hard to miss something like that. No wonder his back hurt so much. What was it, some sort of flagellation deal? He'd had to look at himself through one of the stackroom's cameras to read it. Scarred onto his back in deep, angry cuts, six letters. A word. *Chosen.* Chosen for what? The guy was weird, no doubt about it. Simms was lucky to be alive. But what should he do? Run? Hide? Play along? He had no idea what game they were even playing.

He'd worked out what *Megiddo* was pretty quickly. Nothing obscure there: Megiddo meant Armageddon. The end times when the forces of good and the forces of evil would do final battle and blah blah. OK, so Jones thought this was approaching. Religious nuts were always predicting the end of the world but to date not a single one had been proved correct. But what did any of it have to do with Simms? Jones had talked about soldiers gathering. Was Simms supposed to fight for them? It seemed pretty unlikely. Hard to see how a godless genehunter could be a soldier of the forces of righteousness. No, they obviously needed someone's DNA. He just couldn't think whose.

He knocked his shot back. Maybe he should tell Ballard everything and let the GMA sort it out. Problem was, Simms was bang in the middle and the GMA weren't going to put any effort into protecting him when the firing started.

The hell with it. He should get on with The Zombies of Death. Do his thing, track down the DNA and not worry about anything else.

He stood and strode out of the bar into the mist of a San Francisco morning, enjoying the fug of intoxication in his brain. And, instead of doing any of what he'd decided, he pinged Kelly.

Two days later, Simms stood in the shadows watching Raul Cahn emerge from the Hong Kong Harbour public jump node. 8:02 AM. Bang on schedule. Cahn would walk for thirteen minutes through the thronged streets to arrive at MegaMeta's gleaming harbour front office at exactly 8:15. Simms had hacked into the archives of the local street surveillance system and tracked Cahn's movements for a month back. Cahn didn't depart from the schedule once. It was good to know you could rely on some things. The man could have jumped directly to his private node on the top floor of his tower, sure, but he liked his morning walk, his little routine. Here was someone who didn't ever need to walk a street or breathe the air normal people did. Fortunately for Simms, he still liked to keep in touch with reality.

Simms didn't have to shadow him through the jostling crowds. Instead, he cut through a narrow, winding alley, tall walls on either side that seemed to meet overhead, to wait for Cahn on a carefully selected corner. While he waited, Simms breathed in rich smells from the rows of street food-vendors. His stomach grumbled. Once this little meeting was over he'd eat. Right now, he had work to do.

He waited for the perfect moment, then stepped forward.

"Mr. Cahn. My name is Simms, DNA Detective licensed by the GMA. May I have a word?"

Cahn barely broke step. His eyes narrowed into a scowl and he kept on walking. "Why the hell would I want a word with you?"

Simms caught him up, strode alongside like they were old pals.

"I'd like to discuss something of mutual benefit."

"Yeah? Well I haven't employed a Genie and I can't imagine one is interested in my DNA, so leave me alone."

"I'm sorry, Mr. Cahn. I can't do that."

"Yes, you can. It's real easy. You just stop walking and

talking."

"But what about Alex, Mr. Cahn?"

That got him. Cahn stopped in his tracks. He still wore the same angry, no-time-to-talk-to-inferiors look, but Simms had seen the flash of fear in his eyes.

"Who is Alex?"

"Really, Mr. Cahn. There's no need for pretence. Alex is your two-year old son by your ex-lover, Galena."

Cahn turned on Simms now, grabbed his arm with an iron grip.

"I don't know anything about… such a person."

"And neither does your wife, nor your children. Your other children. You should know I have Galena and Alex's DNA from the records of the discreet Beijing hospital she gave birth in. I have your DNA from a glass you drank from at the Sunset Bar last night up on Victoria Peak. My tests show there is no doubt about the paternity."

Sometimes it was fun to hunt the living rather than the dead.

"What do you want from me?" said Cahn, loosening his grip a little.

"Like I said, I think we can help each other. I have a little problem you can assist me with and in return I can make sure this news doesn't get out."

"And why should I trust you to do that?"

Cahn spoke quietly, not wanting passers-by to overhear, but the venom in his voice was perfectly clear. Simms could understand how it was this man had clawed his way to the top of MegaMeta.

Simms shrugged, like it was of no consequence. "I guess you have to weigh up the odds, don't you Mr. Cahn? You have to ask yourself what gives you the best chance of keeping all this secret. Helping me, or not helping me."

Cahn thought for a moment. Simms could almost see him working through his options. Deny everything. Have Simms killed. Come clean with his loved ones. Eventually he came to the only sensible option open to him.

"And what, exactly, is this little problem I can help you with?"

"I'll tell you the story while we walk to your office. Don't worry, you'll still get there by 8:15."

"Start talking."

"OK," said Simms. "Late-twentieth century punk rock band *The Zombies of Death*. Heard of them?"

"Can't say I have."

"Their bass player was a woman called Stella Stiletto. Not her real name you understand."

"So?"

"I have been legally contracted to acquire the DNA of Ms. Stiletto."

"What has any of this to do with me?"

"Forty years ago, long after the death of the original Ms. Stiletto, she was cloned. This was in the early days of DNA collecting, when the practice was completely unregulated. A collector interested in beat-era musicians acquired her DNA from a hair follicle and recreated her. The DNA sample used has since been lost. Unfortunately, so has the second Ms. Stiletto."

"And what happened to her?"

"Ah, you see that baffled me for some time. She just disappeared one day. She was jumping from London to Paris for a party but never arrived. The police investigated, of course, but found nothing. Eventually it was assumed she'd been abducted and was declared legally dead."

"Sad story. So what?"

"Here's where it gets interesting. She jumped from London to Paris using jump infrastructure owned by MegaMeta."

Cahn shrugged. "Billions of people have used our infrastructure. Literally billions. What does this matter to me?"

"It matters because I've seen the logs of the journey and they're quite clear. Ms. Stiletto entered the jump network in London but never materialised at the other end."

"Nonsense. You can't prove any such thing."

"Ah, but I can." Simms sent over what he'd unearthed to Cahn. It had been surprisingly easy. Social engineering of employees got you a long way. Bribery and hacking took care of the rest. The sheer volume of data probably put most investigators off, but Simms had been persistent and had good AI routines.

"It's just a mistake," said Cahn. It hardly matters now. It's ancient history."

"Except it's not if she's still in there, is it?"

"What?"

"Come on, Mr. Cahn. Everyone knows it happens. People get trapped in the network. Glitches in the system, human error. Whatever the cause, eventually people are in there so long you don't dare pull them out for fear of the compensation you'll have to pay."

"That's a lie."

"Of course you would say that. Which means I'll just have to pass the information I have about Alex to your wife and our dealings are at an end. Goodbye, Mr. Cahn."

Simms turned and walked away. He just couldn't help himself.

"Wait."

"Mr. Cahn?"

"I can promise you nothing. If there was such a mistake it may have been… rectified years ago."

"You mean you may have quietly pulled her out of the network and killed her."

"We don't do things like that, Mr. Simms."

"Right. You're the good guys. Well, you'd just better hope that's true. Otherwise I'll have to tell your wife she needs to put some new names on her Christmas card list."

"I'll let you know if we can locate Ms. Stiletto."

"I want to be there when you pull her out. I want her DNA."

Cahn's eyes narrowed. Simms could see the controlled

anger in him.

"Very well," said Cahn.

"Excellent. I'll give you twenty-four hours to be in touch. If I don't hear anything by then the information on Alex will be sent automatically."

Cahn nodded.

"Oh, and Mr. Cahn? You should know I won't be using your infrastructure any time soon. Just in case you were thinking of arranging another little glitch."

XX

While Simms waited for Cahn he tried Kelly one more time. Devi too. Once again, neither replied. He hated that. He needed Devi for the DNA of the two more famous band members. He needed Kelly for… what? He couldn't put it into words. But he had to speak to her. If she didn't get back to him he'd jump over there again and start making demands.

While he waited, he researched Forty Days some more, trying to work out what they were doing. What Boneyard was and why it involved him. What did Jones mean, it *will be* a place? The sharp pain in his head nagged away at him as he worked. The cut was deep. His back continued to sting, too, despite the analgesics his plug-in threw at it. Some chemical making it burn constantly. It was like they wanted it there as a constant reminder. He wasn't going to forget Jones and that crucifix in a hurry. Question was, how much should he research them? They were testing him, that was clear. But for what? To see if he came looking for them or to see if he didn't? Perhaps he was supposed to have faith and simply wait.

Simms snorted with amusement at the idea and turned his attention to the *Zombies of Death* drummer, Mayhem. The final piece of the jigsaw. He had one lead but it was his least favourite sort. It was reliable and would almost certainly yield good DNA. That was the good part. The bad part was that it involved illegally disinterring Mayhem's skeleton.

Simms spent all his time telling people the popular image of genehunters was wrong. They weren't ghoulish body snatchers digging up remains at the dead of night. Except that, sometimes, they were. He'd done it himself, more than once. The prospect of doing so again didn't fill him with joy. As well as being dirty, unpleasant work, it was dangerous. Too easy to be discovered. If the GMA found out – or the regular authorities come to that – he was in big trouble. Give him a nice, clean electronic sample any day.

He spent twelve hours looking for something, anything, else. Zip. Mayhem had died after a long and happy life, his musical career by then a distant memory. He was buried in his native Glasgow under his real name: Iain McDonald. There could be no doubt it was him in the grave from the records Simms had found. Simms had to hope he hit upon another lead soon. Otherwise he'd find himself jumping to Glasgow with a shovel.

✕

The ping from Cahn came later that evening, pulling Simms away from his research into Mayhem. He was to jump to a MegaMeta facility on the Chinese mainland. Simms thought briefly about not going. Obviously it could be a trap. There was a possibility Cahn had come clean with his family and was now planning something terminal for Simms. But he doubted it. He had done his research carefully. Cahn made a big play of being the safe and reliable family man. Operators of the jump infrastructure had to be whiter than white, absolutely incorruptible. Their systems saw the DNA of most people on the planet at one time or another, and absolute security was fundamental. Cahn had to think about his public image. If the truth got out he'd be over.

Before leaving, Simms opened the safe concealed in the wall of his kitchen. The safe's was tied to his ID and required a biometric scan of his fingertips before it would unlock. Once it had sprung open, he pulled a metal ring from inside and slipped it onto his finger. He had a lot of illegal hardware, but some it was more illegal than others. This was definitely on the *very* illegal list. A contact disruptor was a very effective way of scrambling an enemy's brain plug-ins. You only had to touch their heads with the device to send all their plug-ins misfiring. The problem was, the devices could do the same to the brain as well, even cause permanent damage. Contact disruptors were illegal just about everywhere and being caught with one was a damn good way to get yourself locked up for the rest of time. But sometimes it was worth the risk. Simms' was small and expensive enough to at least look like a chunky wedding ring. It would fool anyone who didn't know him.

Feeling a little safer with the ring on his finger, Simms jumped to the address.

He emerged in an underground storeroom. Bare walls, harsh lighting, no windows. The sort of place people walked into and didn't came out of. Cahn stood waiting next to two other people. Techs rather than security. Behind them stood another jump node, old-fashioned and clunky. Simms could see no weapons and no one attacked him. That was always good. He strode forwards.

"Mr. Cahn. Good to see you again."

Cahn studied him for a moment, then nodded to the technicians. "I can operate the node myself. Leave, now."

The two left without saying anything. When they had left, Cahn spoke again, his voice booming in the echoing concrete cellar. "If we are to proceed with this I need some assurance no one ever finds out. About any of it."

"So Stiletto is still in there?"

Cahn nodded. Simms couldn't help smiling. He hadn't been sure, not at all. It could well have been a mistake in the logs as Cahn had said.

"What assurance can I give you, Mr. Cahn?"

"That's the problem isn't it? Nothing you can say will make me trust you."

"So why bring me here? I could have waited in the comfort of my own home while the pictures hit the public domain."

"Mr. Simms, please. I brought you here because I believe we can achieve an understanding. As you said, we can help each other."

"How so, Mr. Cahn?"

Video began to stream into Simms' head. A room somewhere. A cell, but comfortable-looking, clean. Inside lay a woman, asleep or sedated. Next to her, in a cot, a baby, also asleep or sedated.

He recognized the woman of course. Which meant the baby must be Eloise. His daughter.

"You see, Mr. Simms, we have power over each other. You can cause me some embarrassment. I can kill these two. And I happen to know you would regret that."

Simms looked at Cahn. Would he do it? Sure he would. For once, Simms was lost for words. He'd been about to say he didn't care about them, Cahn could do what he liked. It was the obvious gambit. But suddenly he couldn't say it.

Instead he said, "How did you get to them? And where are they?"

"None of that need not concern you, Mr. Simms. But I assure you once this matter is cleared up they will be returned to the refuge none the wiser."

"They don't know they've been abducted?"

"That is correct. They won't have any reason to think you're to blame."

"I have your word?"

"You don't need my word do you? It's enough for us to be afraid of each other. Mutual fear is really the only sound basis for a trusting relationship."

Simms couldn't tear his attention away from the images of Kelly and the baby. He forced himself to focus. This was a dangerous situation. And not just for him. He felt gulfs opening up beneath him, gulfs in what he'd assumed was solid ground. Kelly and Eloise meant he was vulnerable and would remain vulnerable. It was an unsettling sensation. He was used to meeting risks with appropriate measures: better security, better technology. A problem and a solution. But he couldn't do that with these two. He had no control over them at all, yet they had power over him, even without knowing it.

How had it come to this?

"If they are harmed in any way…"

Cahn held up a hand. "Yes, yes. I understand."

"Then let's get on with it."

"You do realise we don't need to actually materialise this woman? I can simply extract her DNA from the jump system."

"Call me old fashioned, but I'd like to see her in the flesh, know what I'm getting."

"Very well. But one more thing, Mr. Simms."

"Go on."

"Before we proceed I require all the information you have on how you discovered my… situation. I require names, dates, everything."

Simms considered. If he did what Cahn wanted he'd be condemning more than one person. Cahn wouldn't leave any loose ends. Still, it didn't harm Simms.

"Very well."

Simms sent the details over. Cahn nodded after a moment, turned and began to operate the old node. It had buttons, flashing lights, dials, like something from the early days. Simms almost expected steam. Once all nodes had been like this. When the technology had first appeared he'd waited five years before even daring to use one.

A flash of blue light in the node's doorway and a woman appeared, dressed in retro twentieth-century clothing: ripped jeans, leather boots, a top with *buttons* to hold it together. She appeared to be in mid conversation, her mouth open, but as she stepped from the machine she slumped forwards on weak legs. Cahn caught her by the arm. Any jump was disorientating, messing with your balance and spatial awareness. What must it be like to come out of a jump lasting forty years?

The woman sagged to her knees and vomited clear liquid onto the concrete floor.

"Hurry," said Cahn. "Take your sample now."

The woman looked up and around at them, confusion on her face.

"What?" she said. "Who are you? Where is Jean? Is this Paris?"

"You're fine," said Cahn. "Everything is fine. We just have a few tests and then all will be well."

With a practised movement, Simms pulled a sample of blood from her arm. The woman looked up at him in shock as the needle penetrated her.

"What are you doing? Who are you?"

Simms didn't reply. His plug-ins profiled the DNA he'd captured, came up with a good match on Stella Stiletto's known characteristics. He nodded at Cahn.

"All done now," said Cahn. "Let's help you back into the node and you can get to your party in Paris, OK?"

"But who are you? What is happening?"

The woman was still confused, too weak to struggle.

"Once you reach Paris everything will be fine, I promise," said Cahn.

He pushed her back into the blue light. In an electric flash she was gone, just a pattern of digits in the jump network once more.

"What will happen to her?" asked Simms. "Is she dead now?"

Cahn smoothed down his ruffled hair. He shook his head. "As I said, we are not bad people, Mr. Simms. Ms. Stiletto is back where she was. Not dead, not really alive, I suppose. In a permanent state of anticipation you could say. Is that so terrible?"

Simms didn't reply. Was that the fate Cahn had in mind for him? It was all very clean: no body to get rid of. Just a step into a node one day and then… nothing.

"I'd like to go now," said Simms.

"Very well. And I hope I shall never see you again. If any word of this gets out, any mention of Alex, you know what I'm capable of, I think?"

"I do."

"Very well. We have an understanding. Good bye, Mr. Simms."

Cahn watched him, his face expressionless. Simms didn't reply. He hadn't needed his blasters or the disruptor ring after all. But he was acutely conscious he had made an enemy in Raul Cahn. And Cahn wasn't going to let a threat hang around. Sooner or later Cahn would tidy him up as well.

Another one for the list.

Simms stepped into the public jump node. Part of him wondered whether he'd ever step out of it again. But Alex would protect him for a while at least. He tried to forget about Cahn. He had other things to worry about. The baby in the cot, asleep and vulnerable. That, for some reason, was a picture he couldn't get out of his mind.

XIX

Simms scanned the earth beneath his feet, high-def penetrating radar. No point spending six hours digging an empty grave. Clear results came back immediately. Definitely a body down there, fully grown, almost certainly a male judging by the shape of the pelvis.

He looked around. A freezing night in Scotland, the stars twinkling away through the orange glow of the city. A full moon hung in the midnight sky, casting shadows on everything without providing any real illumination. He swore he'd seen a bat earlier, too. Jesus Christ. He wouldn't be surprised if an organ started thundering out minor chords from the unlit church behind him.

He speared his spade into the hard ground and began to dig. With the acquisition of Stella Stiletto, he'd begun to get twitchy. The other genehunter, whoever it was, might be ahead of him. Simms had found no other leads on Mayhem. His competitor would reach the same point and travel to Scotland, too. Simms had to visit the grave. If it looked undisturbed, he was still in with a chance. And then, since he was there, he might as well retrieve the DNA himself.

He just damn well wished Devi would re-emerge so he could trade for the other two band members. Had she gone and gotten herself killed? That would be just like her. He had no Plan B for what he'd do then.

The frozen ground was like stone, jarring his arms as he tried to thrust the spade into it. It would get easier as he got further down. He began to dig, levering up squares of turf then getting into a rhythm of spooning out the soil onto the spoil-heap. His breath billowed out in the freezing air but he soon warmed up. Digging a grave did that.

He fell into a trance while his body worked. He'd rigged up perimeter sensors around the area in case anyone came near. He was safe enough. There weren't going to be many people about in a graveyard at two in the morning in the depths of a freezing winter. Just genehunters and the dead.

He thought about Kelly. Was she OK? He'd tried several more times to get in touch with her. Figured if he didn't it might look suspicious. She hadn't replied, but sooner or later she'd have to. If Eloise was his, Kelly couldn't refuse to talk to him. She was in a difficult situation, too. clONE would not be happy if they learned *he* was the child's father. But he needed to know for sure if he was. A DNA test was the obvious answer. He didn't relish suggesting *that* to Kelly at all.

He heard the footfall behind him even as white light flooded the pit he'd dug. Someone had bypassed his security. That kept happening. Gideon Jones again? He turned, his plug-ins trying to resolve the indistinct figure behind the blinding light. He could make nothing out. Simms dropped his spade and reached for his own weapon. A warning shot thumping into the black soil near his feet froze him.

"Just keep digging, Simms."

"Devi? You're…"

"The other genehunter. Good of you to do all this digging. I'll wait until we've got a good sample from Mayhem's teeth before I kill you, if you don't mind."

"And if I refuse?"

"Then I can kill you now, my friend. After all, you are standing in a grave. Getting rid of your body won't be a problem. I'll miss you or course, but there we are. Business is business."

"So you survived your regeneration?"

The last time he'd seen her she'd been a head and some limbs and not a whole lot in between.

"Good as new. Better, really. Now, if you'd like to toss your weapons up here I'll let you get on with the digging. And don't try anything with your brain hardware either, because it isn't going to work."

Simms considered. She would kill him if she had to, he had no doubt. And the fact she was the other genehunter meant she wasn't going to give him the DNA of the other two band members. Which left him only one thing to bargain with.

"This your first job back?"

"Uh-huh."

"So, you're going to be real keen to make it work, show the world you can still operate?"

"You're not digging, Simms."

"But, ah, you have a problem. Stella Stiletto."

"Already got her."

"No you haven't. Her DNA survived in only one place. I know this because I harvested it yesterday. From somewhere you're not going to be able to get to."

Devi said nothing for a moment. It told Simms everything he needed to know. She didn't have Stiletto.

"I'm not going to deal with you, Simms. I'm the one holding the gun, here."

"And if you shoot me you lose Stiletto's code, too. If I die my plug-ins fry. But no need for that. We can still come to an agreement."

"How so?"

"We'll get Mayhem, I'll give you Stiletto and you can go claim your two million from Lund."

"And you'll do that, what, because you love me?"

"That, of course. And other reasons."

"Which are?"

Simms paused for a moment. Did he really want to do this? He hated to be beaten over the Zombies of Death gig. He prided himself on *never* coming second. But he had too much else buzzing around in his brain. He was making mistakes, leaving trails. He should never have let Devi just waltz through his defences like that. He was too distracted. What he needed was information and if anyone could help it would be Devi.

Slowly, he began to remove his shirt.

"This is hardly the time, Simms."

He didn't reply. Now that'd he'd stopped digging he could feel the freezing night sucking the heat out of him. He ignored it. He dropped his shirt and turned around so that Devi could see his back and read the word carved there.

Chosen.

"Know what that is, Devi?"

"I know."

"How much do you know?"

"Some. Not everything."

Simms turned to face the light again.

"OK. Here's the deal. First, you stop blinding me with that damn light. Second you put your blaster down. And thirdly you come and take your turn at digging up this skeleton. Once we're done I'll give you Stiletto and you tell me everything you know about Boneyard."

"Why should I trust you? Or even believe you?"

"Come on, Devi. We've been here too often for that. I'm not some client you're trying to screw for more money. We're old friends. I don't need to compete with you here. I have bigger problems than The Zombies of Death."

Devi didn't reply for a moment. Then the blinding light cut out and Devi jumped down beside him in the grave.

"Put your shirt back on, Simms. You'll catch your death."

Two hours later, exhausted and filthy, they had their DNA. For all his wild rock and roll lifestyle, the man had looked after his teeth, at least. They each took a copy, although its worth was pretty low to Simms.

"So tell me," said Simms. They sat with their backs against Mayhem's gravestone. In the east, the sky was beginning to shade into purple.

"Give me Stiletto first," said Devi.

He was too exhausted to argue. "Sure. Here you are."

He sent the data over to her, watching her as he did so. She grinned through the mud on her face. She now had the complete genome of The Zombies of Death. She had two million and her reputation back. No wonder she looked happy.

"So," said Simms. "Tell me what you know."

Devi sighed. Simms wondered what she'd do. Maybe she would kill him. He found he suddenly wasn't that bothered whether she did or not. Life was too complicated, sometimes.

"You've been chosen by Forty Days," she said. She sounded almost sorry about it, like it was a blow to her.

"Guess so."

"Are you going to do what they want?"

"I don't know what they want. The guy I spoke to got all apocalyptic, talking about the soldiers of the Armageddon. Why they need me I have no idea."

Devi thought for a moment. "They won't let go of you, you know. You're either with them or against them. And if you're against them, you're dead. They're not big on grey areas."

"But what do they want? Only, if they want me to bring about the Second Coming, that may be beyond even me."

"I don't know what Boneyard is, but I do know about some of the DNA they're after. You're not the only hunter to be employed by Forty Days. You remember we discussed Sanchez? When you came to see me in Cairo?"

"The hunter who went MIA, sure."

"She was *chosen* too. She told me some of it and I pieced the rest together afterwards."

"People do confide in you."

"It's my sweet nature. You happen to know the church of Santa Sofia in Sienna?"

"Can't say it's somewhere I go much."

"You surprise me. Well, if you did go there you'd be able to see the holy relics of the saint herself, where they've been since the fourteenth century."

"So?"

"The relics in questions are actually her severed head, kept miraculously preserved in Holy Water – if you believe what they say – and put on display for the believers to venerate."

"You're kidding."

"No. And that was where Sanchez went. Forty Days wanted her to break in and acquire Saint Sofia's DNA code."

"But surely the church are on the same side as Forty Days?"

"You don't keep up with religious affairs much do you?

Forty Days have been declared apostates by the Vatican."

"So Sanchez died in the attempt?"

"Sanchez *failed* in the attempt. The dying, that came later. When Forty Days learned she'd let them down. They'd chosen her and she had the temerity to fail them. Bad move."

Simms didn't reply, lost in thought. Forty Days were collecting *saints*? They were Jones' soldiers? That was Boneyard? It was crazy. Just what battle were they going to fight? Simms tried to make sense of it all, see it from the viewpoint of someone like Gideon Jones. Tried and failed. It was madness.

He had to admit, though, it was a hell of a gig.

Eventually, Devi put a hand on his arm. "Come on. Let's get this grave filled before the nice people see what we've done."

He nodded.

"And Simms? Be careful, yeah? You'll be no fun if you're dead."

Simms nodded again, stood and reached for the spade.

※

"Citizen Simms? You are under arrest for the illegal possession of unregistered brain enhancement plug-in technology."

Simms could only stand and stare at the three uniformed police troopers who had stopped him on the London street near his stacktower. It was rare enough to see one of them, despite everything that went on. To see three at once was unheard of. And for them to be wasting their time on a good citizen like him was laughable.

Ballard. It had to be Ballard. Of course. A message. *I'm here, I'm watching you, I can do what I like to you.*

"I don't have any unregistered plug-ins, officers."

The leader of the three regarded Simms through insectoid sunglasses, a scowl on her face. "Which of course you would say. Are you going to come with us or do I have to RC your brain and force you?"

Simms sighed. He still had Scottish soil on his hands. He needed to sleep. Needed to think. He needed anything but this. But he didn't have a whole lot of choice. Taking on the forces of law and order in the street was not a good idea.

"OK. Let's get this over with."

They walked for forty minutes, down towards the river and the large, concrete building on the Embankment that housed this regiment of the police. The walk amused Simms at first, the way everyone scuttled out of their way. No wonder the police were paranoid. It soon became boring, though, and he was relieved when they reached the building. The officer with the eyes pushed him into a holding cell. Another small, square room.

Simms lay back on the wooden bench. He practically felt at home in places like this.

XIX

He always figured he'd be able to handle solitary confinement. He could take or leave other people. But after twenty-four hours of waiting he was beginning to have doubts. They'd fed him a couple of times and he'd pounded on the door and shouted more than once, suddenly terrified he'd been forgotten. At the same time he knew it was all part of the game. He just had to wait, not let them win. Good entertainment plug-ins helped. At least it gave him chance to think about everything that had happened. He wondered what Devi was doing with her money. He wondered about Kelly. He tried to ignore the creeping fear in his stomach that Cahn hadn't returned her to the refuge.

Finally, the door was pushed open with a hollow *clang*. Simms pretended not to notice for a moment, like the whole thing was a bore. Finally, he opened one eye.

A man he didn't recognize stood there, flanked by two grim-faced guards. The sort that attacked first and didn't bother asking questions afterwards. Simms scanned the man's plug-ins for an ID. What he got came as a shock.

Simms hauled himself to his feet. "Ballard? That's you? What the hell happened to your face? You look almost human."

The features that normally dripped like a melting candle were gone. Ballard looked handsome. Square-jawed, clean-shaven, clear-eyed.

"I look as I need to look, Simms. Right now I need to look like this."

So, Ballard was a face-changer. That made sense for a GMAn. He'd be able to take on another person's face and go undercover. The technology was expensive. It wasn't just a plug-in; it was a major piece of metabolic engineering. Osteoblasts and osteoclasts marshalled to alter maxillofacial bone structures. Cranial muscles bulked, stretched or sculpted. Skin pigmentation altered. It was cool stuff.

"And the usual horror show appearance?" asked Simms.

"One I keep just for the low-lifes."

"And this is the real you?"

"Maybe."

"Well, since you're here, what can I do for you, Agent Ballard?"

"I'm told you've been in here a while. My apologies."

"You left me in here deliberately and you know it."

"But that would be illegal."

"Yeah. I should report you to the police."

"Still, now that I've found you, I suppose you may as well tell me how it's going with Boneyard."

Here was one of those moments. Which side was he on? Ballard's or Gideon Jones'? Actually, that was an easy question to answer. Neither. They were as bad as each other. Simms would do what he always did: play his own game, walk a line between them.

He had only one worry. It had nagged at him ever since Jones' visit. Simms had been knocked out for eight hours and Jones clearly knew about plug-ins and brain anatomy. The wound on the back of his head *could* be artificial. Simms couldn't escape the troublesome thought Jones had done something to him in those eight hours. Something else besides the word on his back. Maybe even embedded a hidden plug-in within his brain so they could monitor everything he did and said. He'd scanned himself, sure, trying to identify such an addition. He hadn't been able to find one. But would he be able to?

Once again, he dismissed the thought as crazy. As a boy he'd been a believer, brought up as a good Christian. But the idea that God could see his most private thoughts, knew every stray notion or urge that crossed his mind, had finally relieved him of his belief. It was too creepy. This anxiety about stealth plug-ins was just a paranoid echo of that.

Still, he'd keep Ballard in the dark as much as possible.

"OK," said Simms. "Since you happen to be here. I met someone involved with Boneyard. And, just so you're suitably grateful, you should know I nearly got killed in the process."

"How terrible. Still, you survived. What did this person say?"

"You mean, apart from discussing how he was going to rearrange my brain with a sharp piece of metal?"

Ballard waved that aside, as if it was of no consequence. "What did he say that was interesting?"

"Nothing. The usual threats of mindless violence. You know, the sort of thing you come up with all the time."

Ballard stepped forward, grabbed Simms and rammed him against the wall. Simms' head cracked against the hard stone. The pain from half-healed wound on the back of his skull flared back into life momentarily.

"I don't just do *threats*, Simms. Tell me what you found.

Unless you're saying you know nothing. Because if you're no use to me any more I might just forget you're in here permanently."

Simms sighed, trying his damndest to appear indifferent. "He told me nothing, Ballard. Made it clear I should stop asking questions. You, too."

"He mentioned me?"

"Knew you were after them. Said I was to tell you to stop."

"You recorded this conversation?"

"Sure. But all the recordings have been wiped. From my brain and everywhere else."

"You expect me to believe that?" Another shove, another ringing crack on the back of his head. Still, the pain took his mind off all his other aches.

"I don't care what you believe, Ballard."

"You think you can string me along, don't you Simms? Make up some story and I'll leave you in peace, is that it?"

"It's not a story. Trust me, I wish it was."

"Prove it."

Time to show Ballard what Jones had left. Give the GMAn enough to keep him sweet, that was all he had to do. Was that why Jones had left it?

"OK, there's this."

Simms sent over the single frame that was his only remaining electronic record of the visit of Gideon Jones. It had clearly been left in his brain for a reason. Perhaps Simms was supposed to keep it to himself and perhaps he wasn't. He didn't really care. He needed to give Ballard something.

There was a pause while Ballard examined the image.

"Check the timestamp on it," said Simms.

"Could be faked,' said Ballard. "It could all be faked."

"Analyse it all you want, you'll see it's genuine. No enhancements or fabrications of any kind. There's me lying on the ground and there's the messenger sent by Boneyard."

"Did he have a name?"

"Said his name was Gideon Jones. Mean anything to you?"

Ballard ignored the question. "What is he doing to you?" Ballard asked, still inspecting the image in his mind, something like revulsion in his voice. "He's operating or something."

"Yeah. A picture can be spoofed, maybe, but wounds can't. Look what he's doing with that sharpened crucifix."

"He's cutting into your back. The marks look like… letters."

Simms pulled up his shirt once more and turned round to show Ballard.

"*Chosen*," Ballard read. "What does that mean?"

"Too difficult a word for you?"

"Don't get smart with me, Simms. It doesn't suit you."

Simms turned to face Ballard again. "So you think I'd do this to myself?"

"You might. Who knows what you get up to in your spare time. But assuming you didn't, what the hell does it mean?"

"He didn't say what I'd been chosen for or, if he did, I have no recollection of it. But he didn't kill me, so they must want me for something."

"Maybe," said Ballard. "You're sure you have no memory of any conversation? What you may have been chosen for?"

"Nothing. Ream my brain if you like. I know you enjoy doing things like that. But trust me, I've tried and failed to find any records. We talked about something, he knocked me out, carved this on my back, then left."

"At least, you hope he did it in that order," said Ballard. "So if this guy was sent by Boneyard, did he say who Boneyard was?"

Mac had said Boneyard was a thing, not a person. Ballard really was in the dark. Best he stayed that way. "No. So, you just going to leave me in here, Ballard? Or do you want me to go out there and do my damn job? Which, despite all the terrible risks I'm taking, I'm prepared to do for the sake of our friendship."

Ballard regarded him for a moment, considering. "Get the fuck out of here, Simms. And next time you get something, tell me, OK? Don't make me come and find you again."

Simms pushed past him towards the cell door.

"Of course, Agent Ballard. Whatever you say."

XIX

The knock came on his stackroom door two weeks later. Simms had been expecting it. He'd spent a big chunk of the Tom Jacks money enhancing his security systems but once again none of them warned him. Simms opened the door to Gideon Jones once more, tensing for another EM onslaught.

No attack came.

"Mr. Simms. Good to meet you again."

"Is it?"

"May I come in?"

"Is there any point me saying no?"

"Not really. But politeness costs nothing."

Inside, Jones cleared another space on Simms' couch with a gloved hand, like he was afraid of being contaminated. He sat and looked at Simms.

"I hear you've been talking to Agent Ballard of the GMA."

Did they know what he'd said? What he'd thought? But if they did, why were they even here?

"I answered some of his questions. I chose not to mention *Megiddo*."

Jones held up his hand. "Please, Mr. Simms. We are well aware of what was said. And what wasn't said."

"You're unhappy at having your image passed to the GMA?"

"Not really. As you calculated, we gave you that image for just this purpose. We have no desire to jeopardize your close connection to the GMA. It could be useful."

So were they monitoring his thoughts? They seemed to know them pretty damn well. Was that really possible? In case it was, Simms tried not to let the image of what he'd really like to do to Jones form in his mind.

"Useful for you or me?"

"Perhaps for both of us. In any case, can you be sure you gave them my true likeness?"

"It sure looked like you."

"My point is, how do you know what you are now seeing is reliable?"

"You're saying you're in my head, fritzing with my plug-ins?"

"God sees all."

"Maybe. But you're not God."

"I'm rather closer to him than you are."

"Look, why are you here?"

Jones stood, strode around the room, picking his way carefully around the piles of clothes and old plates of food lying around on the floor.

"You're a sinner, Mr. Simms."

"Yeah. You mentioned that. And yet here you are, giving me information. Sounding me out. It's almost like you need me for something."

"You're evil and you're unrepentant. But even someone such as you should have a chance of redemption."

"So you do want to employ me."

"You learned about Megiddo?"

"Sure."

"When the end comes we will all be judged, Mr. Simms. The final day. And if you help us, perhaps you will be admitted into His arms and find eternal bliss."

"I'd rather you just paid cash. If you don't mind."

"What does money matter? I'm offering you the chance to avoid eternity suffering the tortures of purgatory."

Simms was beginning to feel a little happier. They did need him for something. "Look, I don't really care who or what or where Boneyard is. Whatever the big, scary secret is, it no doubt makes sense to you. So just tell me what DNA you're after and I'll see what I can do."

Jones watched him for a moment, saying nothing. Debating with someone remotely? Praying? You couldn't tell which with people like this.

"You've done well so far, Mr. Simms. Perhaps we can trust you after all."

"So I'm *chosen*, right?"

Jones smiled for the first time. "Perhaps. We'll be in touch, Mr. Simms. Keep yourself prepared. A chance for you to save your immortal soul and, while you're about it, save the whole world."

"How can I refuse?"

"Just so. Now, it's time for me to leave again. Please lie down while I knock you out."

"Is that really necessary?"

"I think so. Otherwise you'll attempt to pursue me."

"I promise I won't."

"And I don't believe you. Now lie down or fall down. I really don't mind which."

Simms considered for a moment, then lay down. Whatever this Boneyard deal was, it was something big. And the simple truth was he wanted to be there when it happened. He wanted to be the genehunter whose name was on it.

"Just spare me the tattoo this time, OK?"

"Oh, but you haven't even found them all from last time yet."

"Huh? What do you…"

But before he could complete the question, blackness flooded through Simms and he knew no more.

3 – THE CLONE WHO DIDN'T KNOW

Simms plummeted from the top of the stacktower. The cracked, grey concrete of the deserted London street rushed up to greet him like an enthusiastic puppy. As he cartwheeled through the air, arms flailing, his brain plug-ins measured the precise distance to the approaching ground, performed a simple calculation and presented their conclusions to his conscious mind. He had 4.5 seconds to live.

His main emotion was relief. He'd feel no real pain as he hit; his cranial hardware would see to that. And then all his troubles with Kelly and Ballard and Gideon Jones and the whole damn lot of them would be over. He felt weirdly calm, almost like he wanted it. Was that it? Had he suspected this was going to happen? He should have been suspicious when the client insisted on meeting at the top of a deserted building. Hell, he *had* been suspicious. Still he'd gone along. Told himself the client had seen too many old movies. He'd made sure the guy was alone, unarmed, yada yada, then like an amateur handed over the DNA he'd been employed to track down.

And the client, instead of wiring across the money, had detonated the explosive charge he'd rigged, hurling Simms over the side of the building.

He would have laughed at how ridiculous it all was if not for the rushing air sucking the breath from him. It hadn't even been a big job. Two hundred K for the DNA of a little-known twentieth century soul diva. It was a doodle, a distraction, a filling in of time. He really was like some rookie no-name starting from scratch. He wondered how much Devi would laugh when she found out. He wondered whether Kelly would laugh or cry.

His last thought was of a baby girl he'd never met. He guessed she'd never know anything about him now.

1.5 seconds. His brain shut down as he flew at the ground.

✖

He was aware of painful white light even with his eyes shut. For the briefest moment he thought he'd made it to heaven after all. Hell, more likely. Or, more likely still, he'd managed once again not to die. A moment of regret washed through him, a sense of burdens being hefted back onto his shoulders.

He squinted open his eyes, the bright light sharp on his retinas. He could make out the silhouettes of three figures standing around him. No wings or horns on any of them.

"Where am I?" he asked. "Who are you?"

Hardly his most original opening. He wasn't at his best. He tried to stand, only to realise he *was* standing, strapped to some sort of metal frame, arms outstretched, completely immobilised. Jesus, didn't anyone just sit you down to talk to you any more?

"Hello, Simms."

A woman's voice, not one he recognized. His plug-ins hailed hers for IDs but got nothing. People were so damn paranoid these days.

"Hi," he said. "So, you saved my life because you wanted the fun of killing me yourself?"

"What makes you think we want to kill you?"

Simms struggled uselessly against his tight bonds. "Seems people keep wanting to."

"Do you know who we are?"

Simms squinted but the light was too sharp. GMA? Forty Days? MegaMeta? Could be any of them. "You're trying to sell me life insurance and this is your sales technique. It's not great, I have to say."

He got an ID from her plug-ins then as she opened up enough to let him see who she worked for. He'd been wrong again. It was the *other* bunch of trained killers out to get him.

"Ah. You're clONE, not travelling salesmen. Easy mistake to make."

His eyes were beginning to work now. The light was still too bright to look into but he could see the square, red tiles of the floor around his feet. They looked familiar for some reason.

"So," he said. "You were walking past that stacktower and caught me? Sweet of you. I'm grateful."

"You hit the horizontal jump node we'd concealed."

"So the client, the guy on the roof...?"

"One of ours, obviously. See, we knew all about you but we needed to be sure. We're not the fanatics people claim."

"Really? Oh, good. You can untie me and I'll leave, then."

"That's not going to happen." Another voice, male, again unknown to Simms. It didn't really matter who any of them were. They were a clONE death squad and pretty clearly that meant they were going to kill him. What he didn't understand was why they hadn't already. What did they want from him? Why the hell did people always seem to want something from him?

"We tested you," the man continued, 'to see if you really would supply the genetic code of Gina Paradiso. So many of your type are incompetent frauds. But you're for real aren't you? A genuine DNA Detective, making your living buying and selling people like they're *things*."

Here it was. The great moral debate. Just what he needed.

"I didn't sell anyone," said Simms, shaking his head. "I sold a bunch of numbers, As, Cs, Gs and Ts in a particular sequence. It wasn't alive. No one died. No one got born for that matter."

"Is that what you tell yourself? To help you sleep at night?" The woman again. He could see her features now: dark hair, young face. She'd be pretty if it wasn't for her angry scowl. Beyond her, plain whitewashed walls. It was hot, too. Damn hot. A dry, desert heat. Lines of sweat trickled down his back.

He suddenly knew where he was. Did Kelly really hate him so much? *This* was her answer to all his attempts to get in touch? His whereabouts handed to a bunch of clONE killers?

"Look," said Simms. "You spend your time defending the rights of clones. So, shouldn't you be thanking me if I help bring more of them into the world?"

He didn't see the fist coming. The woman's blow crunched into his nose. A brief spike of pain hit him before his plug-ins could smother it. Blood filled his mouth.

"You're disgusting," the man said from behind her. "All of you. You think you can treat people as commodities. You're no better than slave-traders, selling DNA to collectors so they can fill their private zoos with living, breathing people. Do you know what happens in places like that? And do you know what happens to those who don't make the grade? The mutations? The rejects?"

Simms shook his head, spat out blood onto the red tiles. "I'm not responsible for the actions of others."

"Then you're either stupid or self-deluded," said the woman.

Simms shook his head again but didn't reply. Without

looking up, he lashed out with an EM attack plug-in, hoping to overwhelm their defences, inflict some pain at least. He was still going to be strapped to a metal frame inside their compound, no one coming to help him, but it might make him feel better.

His attack got nowhere. He looked up to see the three assassins watching him, the man shaking his head pitifully.

OK. They had good hardware, too. No great surprise.

The third spoke now, another woman, older, her ID also unidentifiable. He figured she was the squad leader, standing there at the back and watching. She had long hair: black or dark brown. From the way she stood - poised, balanced - she must be a street-fighter or a dancer. Maybe she was both.

"Tell me, Simms," she said, "Do you think about the people who get made from the DNA you sell? Do you wonder what happens to them?"

He did, of course. What did they think he was? But he had to make a living didn't he?

"Look," said Simms. "We're not going to agree about this. Your job is to hunt down the illegal cloners. Since you seem to include me in that, you'd better get on and kill me now."

"Maybe that's what we should do," said the woman. "But we're not going to. We're going to let you live."

"Why?"

The woman turned away from him and began to pace the room, as if he'd asked a fascinating question she'd never considered. "You are cruel, amoral, pathologically selfish," she replied. "But there are those in our organization who believe you're not beyond redemption."

"Who?"

"Who do you think?"

So this was Kelly trying to *help* him? "And what, I stop genehunting and you let me live out my remaining days in peace and happiness?"

"That would be such a waste of your talents. No, we

want you to track down someone for us."

"You want to employ me as a genehunter? Are you fucking kidding? You're clONE. That's insane. That's against every rule you have."

"Still, we'll release you on the condition you do this for us."

Simms studied the three of them, waiting for the punch line, the sting, the laugh. Nothing came. It looked like they actually meant it.

"Tell me who you need."

The man spoke again now. "We're not entirely sure who he is or what he is. He's definitely alive. We think he's lost, confused, vulnerable. He may need our help. Here's the deal: help him and you help yourself."

"And if I refuse?"

"You know what we *really* like to do to genehunters," said the man.

"I thought I did."

"And we'll be watching you, of course," said the leader. "If you hunt anyone else, even for a molecule collector like Lund, we'll assume our agreement is at an end and come for you. And next time there won't be a hidden jump node to catch you when you fall."

Was this some game they played before killing their targets? He could make out nothing on their faces and got nothing from their brains.

"OK," he said, still expecting them to start laughing at their fine joke. "It's a deal."

No one even smiled. Instead, the older woman sent him details on their target. Just like any regular client except for the not offering payment part. He was more used to dealing in musicians than scientists but, hell, he'd take it.

They untied him and led him outside, through the clashing heat of the Arizona sun to the jump node he remembered from his previous visit. Before he stepped in, he turned to the woman walking behind him.

"Give Kelly a message from me."

"Kelly?"

"Come on, no games. Just give her the message."

"What is it?"

"Tell her she needs to reply to me. Tell her I want to talk about Eloise."

"Who is Eloise?"

"Eloise is none of your damn business. Give Kelly the message and tell her to respond next time I ping, OK?"

Simms turned and stepped into the node. His last conscious thought was that the world had gone insane if you couldn't rely on highly-trained death squads to kill you.

⋈

Simms placed the drinks on the table in front of Devi.

"So, couldn't keep away, huh?" he said. He sat down next to her in their shadowy corner of the Double Helix. Which wasn't hard to do because all the corners were shadowy. "Or did you blow all your money from Lund on well-endowed fleshbots already?"

Devi sipped her scotch and smiled at Simms. "Had to come and see if you were surviving, didn't I? You've been getting weird on us. Almost *moral*. Figured you must be ill."

Simms knocked back a mouthful of Scotch, thinking what to say. He'd been trying to make some progress on the clONE case for two days and had gotten nowhere. He'd asked her here for help. Not for a lecture.

"I traded you the Zombies of Death DNA for hard information," he said. "It made perfect business sense."

"Is that right?"

Simms sat back, trying to find the right words. The warm bite of the Scotch cushioned him from reality. His plugins reacted by implementing the intoxication-handling rules he'd set up, locking out wild or dangerous behaviour.

He let them run. They generally knew what they were doing.

A gentle hubbub of low voices filled the air in the Double Helix. No one near, no one paying them any attention. Mac standing behind the bar watching over everything like a fond parent. They were safe here. Neutral territory.

"A lot of shit going on," said Simms quietly.

"Forty Days. You said."

"That's just the start of it, Devi. I got clONE on my back, too."

"We've all got clONE on our backs, sweetheart."

"Yeah, but I mean *literally*. A death squad stung me, took me prisoner."

"Yet here you are, looking more or less alive. Sometimes I think you make all this stuff up."

"I'm serious. They want me to go over to the fucking *light side*."

"You? Come on."

"Me, yeah."

"And you gonna do what they want?"

"Maybe. Don't see I have too much choice. They were pretty persuasive. Figure I'll give them what they want and keep them sweet, at least."

"Like you always do."

"Like I always do."

The door to the outside world opened then, and two young genehunters barged inside. Little more than boys, laughing raucously at some private joke, shattering the calm of the bar. Simms didn't know them. He'd lost track of all the young guns. And you didn't check out other hunters' IDs here in the Double Helix. That was the code.

He looked away. He didn't need to know who they were; he knew their *type* well enough. Brash, ruthless, aggressive. No finesse. That was how the kids were these days. Maybe he'd been the same, once, but he'd learned a few things since then. He was willing to bet neither of these punks had been visited by Ballard or Gideon Jones or been snatched by clONE. Maybe if they had they'd be a bit less cocky. He shook his head. They were just children, unimportant.

He looked back at Devi who was studying him, eyes narrowed. She wouldn't need brain plug-ins to guess what was going through his mind. They'd known each other nearly ten years. They'd had flings, on and off. Sometimes they were mortal enemies and sometimes they were lovers. On a couple of occasions they'd been both at the same time.

"There's more, though, isn't there?" she said. "You got the religious weirdos and the clone lovers and the GMA all gunning for you, but there's something else too, right?"

Simms shrugged. "There's always something else."

"You're trying to find the words to tell me you love me?"

Simms ignored her. "See, Devi, I got all these scary groups with guns and shit coming after me, but I *understand* them. I know how to deal with them."

"So what *don't* you understand?"

"You remember Kelly?"

"How could I forget my rival for your affections? The raven-haired beauty with the liquid eyes. Actually, now I come to think of it, I should have gone with her rather than you."

"Yeah. Good luck with that."

"So, you're not over her. And there she is, on the side of the angels, tearing you in half."

"No. I mean, yeah, but there's more."

Devi regarded him for a moment. "Ah, so there is a baby."

"You fucking *knew?*"

"I heard rumours. Not the same thing. It's yours?"

"So far as I can tell. Which isn't very far because I can't get close."

"And you *want* to get close? Seriously? I had you down

as the sort who'd turn and jump half way round the world. I mean, come on Simms. You're hardly parent material. You're hardly a good role model."

He sipped his drink, didn't reply, didn't look at her.

"Sweet Jesus," she said. "Simms the loving parent. Maybe Forty Days are right and the end-times are upon us after all."

"I need to know she's safe is all. Both of them. I'm a danger to them because of what I am."

"Someone's threatened them to get to you?"

"Maybe."

"And you figure if you keep clONE sweet you can earn access to Kelly and your daughter and make everything better."

"Yeah. Plus they won't come looking for me with a rocket launcher."

"You could forget all about them, you know. Change ID, come and have some fun with me. We could see if your stamina has improved any."

He shook his head. That was what he *should* do. He just damn well couldn't. However he tried to distract himself a little part of his brain whispered away to him, worrying about Kelly and Eloise. It was like he was haunted or something.

"And say you do all this," said Devi. "What happens after you get the girl?"

"What do you mean?"

"Come on, Simms. You'd get bored within a week without genehunting. You're always saying that. You're not cut out for anything else."

"Yeah, well, maybe I should go over to the other side, hunt the genehunters for kicks instead."

"You? Join the GMA? Run around following Ballard's orders?"

"I'm talking about clONE. Kelly went over to them. I could too. Maybe that's what they want. I could see myself heading up a death squad. The righteous fervour of the convert. Could be fun."

The truth was the thought hadn't crossed his mind until that moment. As he said it he didn't know if he was serious or not. By the look on Devi's face she wasn't sure either. But maybe it wasn't such a crazy idea. He'd get clONE off his back. The GMA too. The GMA *liked* clONE, liked their direct approach. There were enough rumours: the GMA men who tipped off clONE death squads because they couldn't get their man and stay within the law. He'd just have to sort out Forty Days and life would be sweet. He'd miss genehunting, sure, but hunting the hunters could be fun, too.

"I thought you liked being the maverick, the lone wolf, walking the line between all these powerful organisations."

Simms shrugged. "You can't beat them, though, can you? Sooner or later one of them will come for you. Might as well pick a side."

"OK," said Devi. "So, you need my help to become my mortal enemy. That about it?"

"I guess."

"Well, you know what? I am gonna help you, Simms. Want to know why?"

"Because you value my friendship so much?"

Devi snorted with laughter. "Because your life is a train wreck. You're a fucking slow-motion *explosion*, Simms. An ongoing disaster. And I want to see what parts of you are left at the end of it all."

"Thanks, Devi. I knew I could rely on you."

"I'd like a full body MRI scan."

The doctor assessing Simms blinked only once before replying. They sat in her cool, cream-coloured consulting room in Sydney Central Hospital. Tasteful pictures on the wall and interestingly elegant ornaments on the shelves. She wrote something on the tablet resting on her knee.

Completely obsolete technology, of course, but it made her look professional, thoughtful. Simms suppressed a smile.

"I see, Mr. Alietev," she said, using the ID Simms had adopted for this little jaunt. "And can you tell us why you would like us to carry out that particular procedure?"

A fair question. He was tempted to tell her the whole thing with Gideon Jones. But she wasn't going to believe it was she? He wasn't sure he believed it himself.

"I need you to look for any anomalies."

"Could you explain what sort of... anomalies we're looking for?"

"Just anything that shouldn't be there."

"Perhaps an object has been... inserted into you?" she prompted. She remained utterly expressionless, professional. Seen it all before.

"No, it's nothing like that," said Simms. "I simply have reason to believe someone has left a message within my body."

"A message."

She couldn't help a flash of incredulity passing across her face. Simms was really quite pleased to have surprised her. He'd be a good story for her to tell her colleagues.

"A message," said Simms. "Maybe a single word. I have reason to believe someone has... tattooed... it within my body."

He could see her longing to ask him what had happened, how such a thing was possible. What the *hell* he was talking about.

"But you must have checked yourself?"

"I've checked my skin, of course. I need you to scan inside me."

"You're aware you can't have a *tattoo* inside your body? A tattoo is a skin decoration, ink injected into the dermis."

"Sure. Obviously. Not a tattoo as such. I don't know what you'd call it. I need you to scan me everywhere and look for... anything unusual."

She nodded, looked at him for a moment, wrote some

more. Simms wondered if she was scribbling nonsense to give herself time to think. Maybe she was consulting with someone electronically about the day's weirdo.

"OK," she said finally. "We can do that. And since you're one of our gold customers we can prep you for the scan first thing tomorrow. If you're sure this is what you want?"

Simms nodded. "The sooner the better. And I want copies of all the images you take so I can study them myself."

The doctor looked like she was about to ask why, but restrained herself. "Of course, of course."

"And I also ask that you keep no records of this procedure. In fact I want no trace of my visits at all." She'd think he was paranoid. Maybe she'd be right.

"As you wish. We guarantee complete discretion."

"And while you're scanning me I'd like a full brain plug-in assay."

"You would?"

"I have some suspicion I've been given an implant my normal diagnostic routines have failed to detect. This is... less likely than the message I described, but I would still like you to check."

The doctor said nothing for a moment as she studied him. They had to satisfy themselves any patient requesting treatment was sane. She was clearly having doubts, probably thought he was an alien abduction nut or that he believed shadowy security organizations were trying to track him down. She'd be right there, at least. But she had no choice but to agree to his requests. By any objective measure he was sane. And, more importantly, he was the paying customer.

"Of course," she said finally, smiling a little too sweetly. "We'll be sure to check your brain very carefully, Mr. Alietev."

Devi pinged him as he trudged home through the familiar, sweet rain of London. He'd stepped into the public jump node in Sydney as Gregor Alietev, a software architect from Kiev. By the time he emerged from the jump network he was officially himself again. He liked to switch IDs in the ether like that, figured it would make tracking him more difficult. Probably wishful thinking.

"Devi," he replied as he walked. "That was quick. Nothing better to do with your life, huh?"

"I exist only to please you, Simms."

"Yeah? You don't do a very good job, then."

"You want to know what I've got or you want to fuck off?"

"Tell me. Sure. I'm grateful, really."

A police riot-control tank rumbled up the street behind Simms, blaring its horns at him to get him out of the way, sending crude alarm calls ringing through his plug-ins. Simms turned and stepped backwards from the massive bulk of the vehicle as it loomed over him, yellow lights flashing, guns tracking anything moving. He was more or less at the place Ballard's grunts had apprehended him after the Zombies of Death affair. Was this another little episode like that? Ballard showing him how hilarious his sense of humour could be? Simms tensed, preparing to run. He was in no mood for Ballard's games.

One gun-turret tracked him as the stood there, but the vehicle didn't slow down. It ploughed up the street, trampling anything in its way. It reached a collapsed building, a rough pyramid of broken bricks and plaster spilling into the street. The tank didn't stop, just rolled over the blockage. The streets had been choked with cars before the jump network, the air thick with fumes, and they'd all longed for clean air and quiet streets. Now look at it. Really hadn't worked out, had it?

"Simms? You there?"

"Sure, Devi. Sorry. Go on."

"OK. I got nothing on any extant clones of Dr. Grendel."

"So, what, you're contacting me to gloat?"

"Always. But listen, have you wondered why clONE wants him so much?"

"Not really."

"I think it's weird. You know what the original Grendel was?"

"Something to do with early cloning attempts."

"He was important. Worked on the cloning vat technology. Like, he created it all. At the start of the last century people sometimes referred to clones by Grendel's own term for them: *simulacra*.

"So you think clONE wants to punish all his copies because of what he did?"

"For all I know they want to worship them. I stopped understanding clONE a long time ago."

"But you got nothing on surviving clones?"

"Zip," said Devi. "But I think clONE is right and they do exist. Or did exist anyway."

"Why so?"

"You must know Grendel's reputation. Used to experiment on himself. Cloned himself repeatedly to test out his devices. Mostly it didn't work, in the early days. Later, he had more success."

"But even if those early clones survived they're going to be dead by now."

"Sure. But there may be second or third generation copies still around."

"Why would there be?"

"I don't know, Simms. You want me to do your damn job for you? But I found out something else, too. There's not much in the public domain about Grendel. I don't even know what he looked like. His research was extremely controversial and he went to great pains to stay in the shadows. But there is a surviving grandchild. Maybe she knows something."

"You got an address?"

"I managed to find it by, let us say, talking nicely to the right people."

"You're a bad person, Devi."

"I love my work, Simms. But listen, talking to Grendel's offspring may not go well."

"Why so?"

"His family despised him. He wasn't a nice man. I mean, even *I* think he wasn't a nice man. He didn't just use himself in his experiments."

"His family too?"

"His children, anyone he could get his hands on. A real fucking charmer."

"Maybe that explains any second or third generation clones," said Simms. "Plenty of collectors out there who go for the evil dictators and the Dr. Deaths."

"So I heard."

"OK, thanks, Devi. I got one other thing I need to do, then I'll pay a visit to the offspring. I owe you, yeah?"

"You always owe me. Remember it when you come looking for me with your clONE death squad."

XIX

Simms stood in the shadows at the back of the church of Santa Sofia in Sienna. Sunlight streamed through high windows. The cool interior reverberated to the beautiful harmonies of the choir. He listened for a time, letting a far-away gaze play across his face, like any worshipper or tourist. He pretended not to be watching the door to the crypt.

Of course, he shouldn't be there. If his new friends in clONE found out it wouldn't go well for him. Somehow he didn't think they'd believe him if he said he'd found God. But he had no choice; he didn't live in clONE's simple, black-and-white world. He had Forty Days on one shoulder and the GMA on the other, making their demands. If he didn't do what they wanted he'd wind up dead or locked away for the rest of his life. Somehow he had to keep them all happy.

How did life get to be so complicated? He was just trying to do his damn job.

He'd taken precautions before coming here. To any casual passer-by he wasn't Simms at all. Anyone browsing him for an ID would now see him as Felippe Lombardi, a wine-maker on pilgrimage from the Mezzogiorno. He'd spent good money to download *precisely* the right Italian accent. He had a whole damn life-story worked out: family, job, a villa in the sun-kissed hills. His story was so good he found himself envying the fictitious man he'd created. Lombardi's life seemed so straightforward in comparison to his own.

He waited for ten minutes more, apparently listening to the singing or lost in prayer, before he acted. He walked down the aisle at the side of the church, stepping past soaring gothic pillars, footsteps echoing in the great space. Half-way down he stopped, as any pilgrim would, to cross himself before the holy remains of Saint Sofia. Her head was kept in an elaborately decorated alcove behind thick glass. The reddish-brown water within was murky, making it hard to see details, but she was certainly in there. Impossible to say whether she was flesh or wax. A young woman, her eyes closed like she was asleep. Simms had seen a lot of things over the years but the sight of her sent a shiver through him. She was little more than a girl, looking like she would open her eyes and see him at any moment.

He crossed himself again and walked on. His first plan had been to smash the glass, grab the DNA sample and run. He'd dismissed that pretty quickly. The glass was toughened, five centimetres thick. He could probably come up with a way to punch through it, maybe even get the sample if things went well. The problem would be getting away. The church had top-class security; they took no chances with their priceless holy relics. Simms would be surrounded in moments by security guards with a relaxed attitude to the ten commandments. His chances of escaping would be in the region of zero. Was that what Sanchez had tried to do when she'd been here?

Maybe. And he was only guessing Jones wanted him to acquire Sofia's DNA. But he clearly needed a different approach to the job. A plan B. Something less dramatic but with a chance of actually working.

The wooden crypt door was left open in the day. The church was proud of the vaulted ceilings down there, the carved stone of the medieval tombs. Simms ducked through the doorway and descended the worn, stone steps.

The crypt smelled of dust and wax and the slow passing of centuries. He walked around the maze of rooms, repeatedly ducking under the flanks of the vaulted ceilings. He needed to double-check he was alone, that he hadn't missed someone coming down here. He walked past the gleaming steel door to the subvault, but deliberately paid it no attention. A few paces farther on he paused and pretended to admire the craftsmanship of a carved doorway, stroking the smooth stone. He slipped the tiny video relay into a crevice where it could see the subvault door, then strode on. Twenty metres away, unwatched by any camera he was aware of, stood the stone sarcophagus he planned to spend the next twenty-four hours inside.

The lid was a solid slab of marble. He'd calculated he could budge it if his plug-ins flooded his metabolism with enough adrenaline to kick off glycolysis and amp up his muscles. There'd be tearing and bruising to his tissues, but he could put up with that. It wasn't like he'd be doing much over the next day.

He glanced around once again and set to work, issuing the commands to his brain hardware. The adrenaline rush flooded through him, sending his heart pumping wildly, accelerating his breathing. He heaved on the stone lid with all his strength, grunting involuntarily. It slid a little. Stale air breathed up at him. He couldn't stop. If anyone saw him now he'd be in serious trouble. He hauled again, exposing a triangle of darkness in one corner of the sarcophagus. Inch by inch, he made the triangle big enough to squeeze through.

He climbed onto the sarcophagus and put one leg inside. Bone or stone crunched beneath his foot. So far as he'd been able to tell, the tomb hadn't held a body for several hundred years. Still, he couldn't be sure. He might have to share the sarcophagus with a previous occupier.

He slid his other leg in and squeezed inside, breathing the cold, musty air in short panicky breaths. He lay on a bed of spiky debris, the cuts on his back stinging. It looked like he wasn't alone in here after all. He tried not to think about it. He braced his shoulders against the base and pushed the lid above him closed again. The angle made it more difficult; he could only move the slab an inch before having to stop to catch his breath. Eventually he worked the triangle of light down to nothing. He was alone in the absolute dark. Unless you counted the crumbling shards of bone beneath him. It was just as well he wasn't easily spooked. Or claustrophobic. Or sane.

He knew he'd use up the air in the sarcophagus quickly if he continued to breathe so rapidly. He instructed his plug-ins to reverse the metabolism-boost. Ideally he should let himself come down naturally, but he didn't have the time. His breathing and heart-rate slowed as his body calmed. He wondered what strain he was putting on his organs, how often you could safely pull a stunt like this. He closed his eyes, although it made no difference. He let his core temperature drop and drop towards torpor. He felt consciousness fading. He'd calculated he could last twelve hours like that: cold, barely alive, maybe ten breaths a minute. His brain hardware would rouse him at the right time so he could put the rest of his plan into operation. Of course, if he'd miscalculated how much air he'd have, or if his plug-ins couldn't bring him round, he'd never wake again.

If that happened, would he ever be found? Maybe not for a long time. He imagined someone opening the tomb in the far future, and instead of finding the remains of some medieval noble, discovering a dead man from the twenty-second century with high-tech hardware rattling around in his skull.

His last thought was amusement at what they might make of that.

✕

When he came to, it felt like he *had* slept for centuries. His limbs were lifeless, frozen meat. He could see nothing and had no notion of where he was. For several minutes his world consisted of pain: something spiky digging into his back, a heavy throbbing in his head, ice in his veins. He had no choice but to wait; he knew that much at least. His brain hardware would bring him back to life and soothe his pain when he was strong enough. For now, all he could do was endure.

Finally, full consciousness and understanding returned. He was entombed in the crypt of a medieval church in Italy. OK. He'd had some pretty weird nights over the years, but this one might be the winner.

He accessed the video relay he'd left out there. He could see nothing other than the blinking red lights of the security systems on the subvault door. All well and good. The clock in his brain told him the explosion he'd set up would go off in two minutes. He had only to wait a short time before everything kicked off. He tried to breathe slowly, conserving his air.

He felt the explosion as a faint, muffled *crump* through the stone of his tomb. It was two in the morning; the streets of Sienna would be deserted. Still there would be security guards monitoring the church and its precious relics. Simms had checked over their protocols very carefully. Plenty of people out there hated the church – why, Simms didn't know or care. But the church had systems in place in case of attack. Those measures would now be initiated.

Three minutes later, security guards began to bustle into the crypt, carrying the precious objects from above. Crosses, a vast leather bible, painted statues. They unlocked the steel subvault door and began to place the treasures on shelves inside. They looked like they'd practised the whole exercise many times. Two more guards appeared, carrying the holy relics of Saint Sofia between them. They, too, went into the subvault. Then they emerged, locking the subvault door behind them. That door, Simms knew, was fireproof, blastproof, every-damn-thing-proof. He just had to hope it wasn't genehunter-proof, too.

When the security guards had left, Simms waited another ten minutes in case they'd forgotten something and came back. The air tasted more and more musty as he burned up all the oxygen. Finally he acted. Boosting his muscles once more he pressed upwards with locked arms and pushed at the stone lid of his tomb. It didn't budge. Alarm hammered through him. If his strength had waned too much during his torpor he'd never escape. He tried again, slightly panicky now. Sharp pain shot through his arm muscles, but this time the lid moved, exposing a tiny triangle of grey. He sucked in fresh, wonderful air and, clamping his fingers around the edge of the stone, pulled again and again until he had a gap big enough to squirm through.

He stood for a moment, listening. Nothing; he was alone. His plan was working. Although it was almost a shame there wasn't someone down there to see him. He must be quite a sight.

He crossed through the darkness to the subvault door and set his brain hardware working on the locks. He figured he had plenty of time. The explosion he'd rigged up was small, more noise and sound than anything, but the *Polizia* wouldn't take chances. It should be hours before they gave the all-clear and allowed people back into the church.

While his brain worked on the electronic locks he tackled the physical ones. The key he'd crafted from the X-rays taken two days earlier made that straightforward. Within fifteen minutes he had everything open. Now the problem was the alarm system. If he couldn't disable that, opening the door would bring security running, despite the police's exclusion zone. He probed the electronics, looking for a way to deactivate or spoof them.

Thirty minutes later he gave up. He could see no way. The systems were good, no loopholes or backdoors. Which meant he'd have to go in, work fast and take a chance. He reckoned it would take three minutes at a minimum for someone to get down there.

He hauled open the subvault door and ran inside. He could hear no alarms but knew they'd be ringing somewhere. The reliquary holding the saint's head stood on a stone plinth in the centre of the room. He began to look for a way to open it. He could smash it, but that might damage the sample. He needed to be more subtle. If he was lucky, he could make it look like he'd never been there.

The tiny brass lock holding the clasp in place was useless. Simms sprang it with ease and opened the case. The pungent smell of dilute formaldehyde hit him. So much for Holy Water. At least it suggested the head was real. He acted quickly, pushing a biopsy needle through the liquid and into the skull within. He punctured bone and pushed on for two centimetres, into the brain tissue. He took his sample and pulled the needle out. He had no time to check the sample was good. So long as he got *something*.

He heard banging and shouting from somewhere upstairs even as he closed and locked the reliquary. They were coming for him. Quicker than he'd expected. He dashed from the subvault and began to reengage all the locks. Lights flooded the cellar as he hurried away, fleeing back to the safety of his crypt like some fucking ghoul. He had only a few moments. He pushed himself inside, scraping his shins on the carved stone, and heaved at the lid of the tomb over him. They might hear, but if he left the sarcophagus open they'd be sure to notice. He had no choice.

Putting all his strength into one effort he lifted and pushed. The gap shrank to a tiny corner but he hadn't closed it completely. He heard voices just outside. He didn't dare try to move the lid any more. He had to hope they didn't notice. At least he would have air to breathe.

He waited long moments, not daring to move, expecting the lid to be forced open at any moment. He accessed the video relay. Five guards stood by the subvault door, deep in conversation, gesticulating. One looked around, walked out towards the camera. Simms heard footsteps centimetres from where he lay. The guard stopped. When he spoke, it sounded like he was standing directly beside Simms.

"I thought I heard something over here."

"Like what?" called one of the guards by the subvault door.

"I don't know. A banging sound. A scraping sound."

Simms prepared his weapon. All he could do was try to fight his way out.

"Probably those vampires they keep down here. Make sure you've got your wooden stake ready." The other guards laughed.

"I'm serious. I heard something."

"You're always hearing something down here. You're afraid of the dark, that's your problem."

The guard swore to himself and strode back towards the subvault. Simms lay perfectly still. He watched the guards continuing to debate, the one who had walked over still glancing suspiciously around, the others laughing at him when he did so. Eventually, they seemed to decide they hadn't set the security systems properly and returned upstairs. Once again, Simms was left to the darkness of his crypt.

He instructed his plug-ins to begin suppressing his metabolism once again. Soon, icy torpor reclaimed him.

✕

Twelve hours later, Simms strode from the church into the glorious warmth of the Sienna day. There was little sign of his diversion from the night before, no police anywhere and just a black singe on the ground where his device had exploded. He'd kept the bang as small as he could. There was always a chance Ballard knew about Forty Days' interest in Saint Sofia. The less attention he drew to himself, the better.

He walked across the cobbled square towards the town. His clothes and ID were still those of Felippe Lombardi. His limp was entirely real. His body ached from his twenty-four hours in the tomb and the demands he'd made of his muscles. He needed food and drink and he needed to rest. Somewhere warm and comfortable.

But first, he had one task to complete. He had no real way of knowing what Forty Days expected of him, but he could only assume it was this. He inspected the sample from the head. It looked degraded but it was the best he had. He encrypted it with what he assumed was the key provided for the purpose and sent it out into the ether, to the address he also assumed was provided for the purpose.

The MRI scan had found the two numbers etched onto one of his ribs, right beneath where the word *Chosen* had been cut into his flesh. Tiny digits drawn with some fine, diamond-toothed drill: a twenty-one digit number that looked like a jump address and a sixty-four digit one that might be an encryption key. The whole procedure must have taken Jones hours: he would have had to cut through skin and intercostal muscles to get to the bone, then put everything back together afterwards. Had he done all that, there in Simms' stackroom? The guy was insane, no doubt about it.

Simms was past caring about any of it. He was done with Forty Days now. They were a disappointment, in truth. For all their weirdness and apocalyptic talk they'd ended up being one fairly straightforward piece of DNA collection. He'd imagined this job being one the young punks like those in the Double Helix talked about for years. Something *big*. But beneath all the nonsense about *Soldiers of Megiddo*, there seemed to be nothing more to Boneyard. Gideon Jones hadn't been back in touch. There were no stealth plug-ins in his brain. It was all boring.

Maybe they'd pay him for what he'd done and maybe they wouldn't. That was the way it went. They hadn't even formally employed him, just given him vague clues and left him to join the dots. The hell with them. Simms was at least left with the knowledge he'd done the job, got the DNA. His strike rate remained a perfect 100%, unless you counted the Zombies of Death gig. An anti-climax but there it was.

He just had to hope neither the GMA nor clONE knew about his night's work.

He sat down at a street café in the full heat of the sun and ordered strong, sweet coffee and several sugary, high-fat cakes to bring up his blood-sugar levels. While he sat, basking in the glorious heat, he let his mind go blank.

XIX

"Mrs. Douglas? Can I speak to you?" Three days later, Simms stood shouting through the door of the ramshackle house on the outskirts of London. His attempts to electronically hail the woman inside had gone nowhere. But of course, old people sometimes didn't have even the basic plug-ins. How did they survive? But she was definitely in there. He could hear her pacing about, like she was searching for the best place to hide.

"Mrs. Douglas? Please? I only need a moment of your time."

She'd taken some finding. Devi's address had turned out to be vague: the name of a street. Simms had asked around all morning. Most people hadn't wanted to speak to him. Those that did knew nothing about Dr. Grendel's granddaughter. People liked to keep to themselves. He got that. But eventually, by a process of elimination, he'd tracked her down. The ruined old house, plants growing from cracks in its walls, was the only one he hadn't tried. He'd actually walked past it several times, assuming it was derelict.

An old woman finally answered the door, her face a mass of wrinkles peering through the chained gap between door and frame. Patches of pink scalp were visible through her thinning, grey hair. She was well over a hundred years old if the records were correct. Her eyes focused on Simms and he saw some fire flare up in her. She shut the door, fumbled with the pathetic chain that would keep no one out, then opened the door wide. She looked frail, like she could snap in two at any moment, but before Simms could speak she stepped forward and slapped him hard across his face with a leathery hand.

"You get out of here," she said, genuine spite in her voice. "You're not welcome."

Simms stepped back, surprised. The woman looked like she was ready to strike him again. It couldn't be good for her.

"But you don't know who I am, Mrs, Douglas," he said. "You don't know what I want." She was clearly senile, imagining he was someone from her past. They had never met. Although she did look familiar. Reminded him of someone.

"I know exactly who you are," she said, her voice

quavering. "Go away and don't ever come back. I've told you before."

She shook now, her initial fury gone. She shrank into herself. She would have been tall, once, the same height as Simms, but now she stooped over so that she had to turn her head to peer up at him.

"I'm sorry," said Simms. "But we've honestly never met. I'm here to ask about your grandfather. Dr. Grendel. I'm trying to find out about him."

"You already know everything you need to know."

"I don't know anything, Mrs. Douglas. It appears he was a very secretive man."

"You really don't know?"

"No. That's why I'm here."

The old woman's eyes narrowed, almost disappearing within her skin. Then she started to make a strange noise, great shudders heaving through her body. For a moment Simms thought she was having some sort of attack. Then he realised she was laughing.

"You really don't, do you?" she said.

"I know Grendel was involved in cloning in the early days. I'm trying to find out more about his activities. I believe there may even be some of his clones surviving to this day. Perhaps second of third generation. I'd like to track them down."

"And why would you want to do that?"

"I'm a genehunter. I've been employed to do so."

"Have you now? And by whom?"

"I can't say. But I can assure you my employers want only to help any surviving clones."

The woman looked like she was about to start laughing again. Instead she shook her head and said, "What's you name?"

"Simms."

Now she did laugh once more. "Simms. Very good. You don't even get the joke, do you?"

The old wreck was clearly crazy. His chances of

discovering anything useful from her were slim. Still, he had no other leads. Dr. Grendel was proving to be a very difficult target to track down.

"Please. If you can tell me anything it could be very useful."

The woman stopped laughing and looked serious. He couldn't keep up with her mood switches. "I'll tell you this," she said. "So far as I know there is only one surviving clone of that evil bastard running about. The rest are all dead." She took a step towards Simms and prodded her finger into his chest. "And if I had my way, the last would be killed, too."

"You didn't like your grandfather much?"

"Didn't meet him, did I? Not the original. But I met his genetic twins and I know all the stories of what he did, what he was like. My mother told me everything. Pure evil he was. I almost feel sorry for any clone of his, going about knowing what they've come from. Now, leave me alone and don't ever come back, understand?"

The woman stepped back into the gloom of her hovel and slammed the door in Simms' face. He could smash it back open, sure, but there didn't seem to be much point.

"Please, Mrs. Douglas," he shouted after her. "Can you tell me anything? Can you tell me what you know about this surviving clone?"

The door remained shut. He could hear the woman's slow, shuffling footsteps receding from him, the sound of her muttering to herself. Simms swore. What should he do now? He turned to leave, but stopped when he heard the old woman's footsteps approaching once more. Perhaps she'd forgotten everything that had happened already and had come to see who he was.

"Mrs. Douglas?"

The door opened, back on its chain. This time the old woman held out a square of card.

"If I give you this I want your word you'll never come anywhere near me ever again. Understand?"

"Sure," he said. He had nothing to lose.

Simms took the piece of card. The woman slammed the door closed. Standing there on the step, Simms looked at what he'd been given. It was an old photograph, the colours faded now. It showed a man in an old-fashioned suit sitting behind a large wooden desk. His fingers were poised over the keyboard of an ancient, bulky computer. The man scowled at the camera as if disapproving of it. Writing beneath the picture identified him as Dr. Grendel, Professor of Genetics at London University. But it was the man's face that really caught Simms' attention. He stared at it for a long time, cold dread seeping through his insides.

✕

Simms materialised in the familiar, plain reception room of the Arizona refuge. As before, a disembodied voice spoke to him, its metallic tones echoing in the empty space.

"Please state the purpose of your visit."

"I need to see the clONE hit squad who captured me four days ago."

"Please provide the names of the individuals you wish to see."

"I don't know their fucking names, do I? Just speak to someone from clONE. I know they're here. They'll know me. And tell Kelly, too, if she isn't one of them."

"Please wait, Mr. Simms. Someone will be along to collect you soon."

After several minutes, the door from the outside opened and the woman who led the hit squad stepped into the room on a rush of desert heat. She strode towards him with her dancer's grace, like she could twirl him a roundhouse kick any moment. She assessed him for a few moments, not speaking. Simms returned her stare.

"So, you found the DNA we wanted, Simms?"

"I found it."

"And are you prepared to… hand it over to us?"

"Is that what you want me to do? Or has all this been some elaborate game for your own amusement?"

The woman sighed, looked out through the window, then back at him. "Tell me, how does it feel? Knowing you weren't brought into this world because two people loved each other, or because someone longed for a precious child. But because, as you once put it, you're made up of the right *bunch of numbers?*"

"How do you think it feels?"

The woman nodded. "Let's go for a walk," she said. "Do you mind the heat?"

"I can take the heat."

They stepped out into the glaring furnace of the sun. Through narrowed eyes, Simms could see the houses of the refuge's inmates, looking just like they had that first time he'd come. Was Tom Jacks there? Had he ever been? It barely mattered now. It all seemed like a long time ago. The woman turned onto a different path and led him towards a smaller cluster of low buildings.

"We very nearly told you the truth, you know," the woman said. "*Help him and you help yourself.*"

"Yeah, great. I love a puzzle. You could have just told me."

"Would you have believed us?"

"Probably not."

"You gave us an interesting dilemma, you see. We despise the cloners and the genehunters who help them. We're also sworn to defend the rights of clones to be themselves, do whatever they want to do. To transcend their genetic backgrounds and be free individuals."

"Yeah, I get it. Hence the funky spelling of clONE."

"So, in other words, we protect people like you from people like you. I mean, what are we supposed to *do* with a genehunter who is also a clone? Especially one who is a clone of *him*. In truth we really didn't know what to do."

"And what have you decided?"

"It depends on you, on what you do now. If you carry

on as before we'll pursue you. You've had a fair warning; we've given you a chance to change. After this you're own your own. Understand?"

"And if I change?"

"Then we won't pursue you. If we're convinced about you."

"Now you sound like Forty Days offering me the chance of redemption."

The woman glanced at him, eyes narrowed. "We're nothing like Forty Days. Nothing at all. Have they been talking you?"

Simms wondered what he should say. He shook his head.

"Take my advice and stay clear of them," the woman said. "They're dangerous people if you cross them."

"And you aren't?"

The woman scowled before replying. "Make your choices, Simms. Decide what you want to be then face the consequences, OK? We're giving you the freedom to do that."

"I'd like to see Kelly now. Please."

There was a pause while the woman communicated brain-to-brain with someone. Then she spoke again.

"Very well. She says she'll see you. I hardly need tell you she can summon us in a moment if she needs assistance."

"You don't need to worry about her. Kelly can look after herself, believe me. She's no innocent."

The woman held up her hand. "Please, Simms. We know what Kelly used to be. But she's changed. You can too."

The woman led Simms to one of the small houses in the compound. Some irrigation system had been set up here; the houses were clustered around a little oasis of sparkling water, the green fronds of some tree dipping into it. Standing in the doorway of one of the houses, dressed in a white cotton dress, stood Kelly. She looked well, the sun lighting her up. Last time he'd seen her she'd been lying in Cahn's cell, she and Eloise, the two of them sedated. Did she know anything about that? Those hours she'd mysteriously lost just so the Director of MegaMeta had his bargaining chip? Probably best he never asked her.

"I'll leave you alone," said the woman. Simms walked around the pool of water towards his ex-lover.

"Hello, Simms."

"Hello, Kelly."

"You found out, then?" she asked. "You and Grendel."

"When did you know? When we were together?"

"No, no. When I came here. They told me very recently. You must be feeling confused."

He looked at her, looked away, suddenly not knowing what to say. At least she wasn't so mad at him anymore.

"I… I don't know who I am any more, Kelly. Am I Grendel? Or me? I had parents, a family, everything. Except, now I know it was all a lie. False memories. I don't know who's done this to me. I don't know why."

She looked sorry for him. "I don't know either. But I think you're *you*, not him. You've always been you. A free individual. You're not destined to be like him."

"But I am like him, aren't I? I know what I am. Is that how I'm going to end up? Despised by everyone who knows me?"

She looked away from him. "Sometimes I think you will. When you're working you can be pretty ruthless. But you don't have to be. It's up to you. You're not a machine. Your genes are just your genes. Molecules. It's what you do that's important."

"So it doesn't matter to you? Where I come from, I mean. It doesn't matter to you that Eloise carries that DNA in her, too?"

"No. A little. I mean, it troubles me, sure. But none of us can help where we come from, can we?"

He looked down at the ground, then back up at her. The sunlight sparkled in her hair. He longed for her to put her arms around him.

"Is she here? Eloise?"

"She's inside. Sleeping."

"Can I see her?"

Kelly hesitated for a moment, then stepped aside, granting him access. Inside the cool, quiet room, Simms could make out the low bed in which Eloise lay asleep, lying on her back, utterly peaceful. The sight of her, oblivious of him, oblivious of everything, seemed to stop Simms' heart.

"I'd like to see her again," he whispered. "Get to know her."

"Perhaps you can," said Kelly, standing behind him. "But I'm not letting Simms the genehunter anywhere near her, understand? You don't care about anyone. You don't even care about yourself. I'll tell her about you, sure, but you're having no access to her unless you change. Unless you damn well grow up."

He didn't reply. He could challenge her, sure, try and get legal access to Eloise. He knew it was futile. Everyone would side with her over a genehunter. And he wouldn't blame them. His life was chaotic and dangerous and most days he could barely look after himself.

"Can I have a picture of her at least?"

Kelly considered, then nodded her head. A picture of Eloise, smiling a wide smile and dressed as a princess, arrived in Simms' brain.

"Thanks."

"What you do is up to you, Simms. I hope you will change but if it's not what you want, don't do it. If it is, this is where we'll be."

Simms nodded, his eyes on their sleeping baby.

Fifteen minutes later, the clONE death squad leader escorted him back to the jump node.

"So will we see you again, Simms?"

"One way or another."

"What does that mean?"

Simms didn't reply for long moments. "I need to know who I am," he said finally. "Who has done this to me. Who made me. If you count that as genehunting then we aren't going to be friends."

"You know, I don't think we'd worry about you doing that. We might even approve. We might even help. If you follow this trail, we both know where it will lead."

He did. A collector's zoo. The sort of place clONE spent their time finding so they could liberate those held inside.

"And what do I call you should I wish to get in touch?"

"You can call me Nemesis."

"Such a pretty name. And if I do this, what happens after? I'd be welcome here?"

"Is that what you want?"

"Maybe."

"Well, we'll see. It's all up to you isn't it?"

)(( )((

He wouldn't miss this climb up the stairs of his stacktower. The unrelenting grey concrete and the smell of stale piss. How come they could maintain a global jump network but not a couple of lifts? Still, it kept him fit.

As he climbed, his mind teemed with plans. He had a decision to make. Except, he knew he'd already made it. Genehunting had been fun. Now it was time to move on, do something else. It wasn't like it was his destiny or anything. For one thing, he could go somewhere the sun actually shone and wasn't some distant folk-memory. He'd had enough of rain.

He'd tell Ballard what little he knew about Forty Days and Boneyard. Then he'd be free to find out about his past. Find out who he was. And then, maybe, he could win

Kelly's trust. Or maybe do something else completely. He could do whatever he damn well wanted, couldn't he?

As he approached his stackroom, a little out of breath, he automatically checked ahead there had been no alerts, that all his security was still in place. He was good. His dirty, messed up old room was waiting for him, his only sanctuary in a world of dangers. He'd miss it. He unlocked everything and stepped inside.

"Mr. Simms. Good to see you again."

Gideon Jones sat on the sofa, the same spot as before, the same grey coat and hat and reluctant smile.

It took Simms a moment to react. "What do you want? How did you get in here? I've already given you everything you asked for."

"Please, Mr. Simms. There's no need for any unpleasantness. We're very pleased with you. You followed our little trail very capably."

"I did what you requested. I don't need payment. You can go."

"I'm sorry, but I'm afraid you don't understand. You see, we've decided to anoint you. Employ you. You are our *chosen* one after all."

"What the hell are you talking about?"

"I'm talking about the sacred DNA we need. You're to acquire it for us."

"Just fuck off, Jones. I'm not a genehunter any more."

"But Mr. Simms, I'm afraid that's where you're wrong. Because that's exactly what you are. And it's time we talked to you about Boneyard."

4 – A SOLDIER OF MEGIDDO

Simms pulled out one of his blasters and levelled it at Gideon Jones. "And I told you to fuck off. I'm not a genehunter any more."

Gideon Jones sat on the couch in Simms' stackroom, wearing the same grey coat and the same grey smile as ever. He didn't look worried. If anything, he looked disappointed at Simms' reaction.

Moving with deliberate slowness, Jones reached into his inside pocket. Simms stepped backwards, targeting Jones' forehead. But instead of a gun, Jones revealed an ovoid, metal case. Saying nothing, not looking at Simms now, he opened it with a *click*. Inside was a swathe of black cloth. A wrapping for something. Jones placed it onto the couch beside him and began to unroll it. Within lay some metal objects. Simms saw what they were: scalpels, syringes, clamps and bone saws, all highly polished. Jones looked back up at Simms. Simms found it hard take his gaze from the medical instruments. Were they what Jones had used on him?

"I'm sorry, Mr. Simms. But despite your promises to clONE you remain a genehunter. A remarkably good one. And now we'd like to employ you properly."

Simms thought about pinging Ballard, telling the GMAn to speed over with a squad of thugs. Jones could answer all their questions about Boneyard given the right encouragement. The idea appealed. At a stroke he'd get both the GMA and Forty Days out of his life. Problem was, Jones would block the message or know one had been sent. Then Simms would be all alone with him and his scalpels while Ballard lumbered on over.

"You can't make me work for you by cutting me up again," said Simms.

Jones looked surprised. "Oh, these aren't for that. I have other means to persuade you. These are in case you refuse and I need to do any... tidying up."

"There is nothing you can do to persuade me."

"I rather hoped you wouldn't want us telling clONE and the delightful Kelly about Sienna."

"They aren't going to believe a damn thing you say."

"Perhaps. They can hardly argue with the video of your little escapade."

"Except I was the only one there..." Simms trailed off. The stealth plug-in. Did it exist after all?

"I see you've worked it out," said Jones. "Yes, we've been watching. The experts who scanned your brain in Australia were, unfortunately, not expert enough."

"I don't believe you."

"We never lie, Mr. Simms. Lying is a sin. I have to say, hiding in that sarcophagus, while sacrilegious, was extremely resourceful." Images began to stream into Simms' brain. The church in Sienna just as he'd seen it. Shafts of sunlight slanting down like the gaze of God. The scene shifting as Simms, in the guise of Felippe Lombardi, began to walk towards the crypt.

There could be no doubt. Jones had him. Motherfucker. Fucking motherfucking motherfucker.

Simms lowered his blaster. He tried to think of a way out, an angle, but drew a blank. If he wanted Kelly and Eloise he had no choice. Was that the plan all along? Set him up so they had this hold over him? Christ, he hated that.

"Why do you even need me?" asked Simms. "You're capable of just about anything on your own."

"You have certain abilities we do not. Contacts. Specialist knowledge."

"That's crap. You could ream everything from my brain and find the DNA you need yourself."

Jones smiled his little, reluctant smile. "A fair point, Mr. Simms. Since we are being so honest, the truth is we know we are asking you to commit numerous sins."

"So it's OK for me to damn my soul to eternal torment so long as you're in the clear?"

"As things currently stand you're going to hell anyway, so it makes little difference."

"And this job. It's not to track down the DNA of Jesus Christ is it?"

Jones' bland demeanour slipped for the briefest moment, a scowl flashing across his features. Simms found he had backed up against the wall. He readied himself for attack. He had goaded Jones too much. He just couldn't resist, could he?

His *Kelly* fleshbot, slumped in a corner of the room, chose that moment to spark into life. Reacting to the movement in the room, some last burst from its dying batteries. It looked up with dead eyes, scanned the room for Simms, locked onto him and smiled its too-wide smile. "I want you, Simms. I want you now. Please. I..." Then its head fell forwards, all animation gone. A dead thing once more.

Jones watched the machine in horrified fascination. He turned back to Simms, anger replaced by something like revulsion. "I need you to acquire some DNA, Mr. Simms. What I don't need is a theological lecture you are not qualified to give." He reached out to straighten one of the scalpels a little. "Do you agree or are we back where we started?"

Simms was in no position to argue. They both knew it. "One last job, Jones. After it I walk away unharmed. And I *stay* unharmed."

"You have my word. I speak only for Forty Days, of course. What the Lord has in mind for you I do not know."

"I also want your word you'll never contact me again. Also that no one – Kelly, clONE, the GMA – no one gets to hear about this."

"They won't hear about it from us."

"And I want this plug-in removed."

"I can transmit self-destruct codes to it now. Once you have completed your labours for us we will destroy the video, too."

"And I should just accept your word on that?"

"There is little certainty in life for a sinner such as you, Mr. Simms. But one is that you can believe everything I say. I told you, I do not lie."

"And I want everything you have on my origins."

"We don't know much. We have your DNA and we acquired that of Grendel thirty years ago. We simply spotted the match."

Thirty years. That had to be relevant. He'd be thirty himself soon. It could be a coincidence, but he'd bet it wasn't. "How did you get my code?"

"We employed a genehunter."

"That's pretty funny when you think about it."

"God made the universe and everything in it, including irony."

"And Grendel?"

"A genehunter called Fuchs acquired him for us."

"Why did you want it?"

"Grendel was an evil man. We make it our business to find out all about such people. Anything else? You haven't even mentioned money."

"Forget about money. I just want all this over with."

"My, my. Perhaps there is hope for you after all. Would

you like me to terminate your plug-in now?"

Simms nodded. He braced himself for pain, imagining a tiny explosion inside the folds of his brain. Instead, his vision blurred and the room lurched around. Random voices howled in his ear. Then his senses settled back down to normal.

"It's gone?"

"It is. Now only God sees your every thought."

"Yeah, right. OK, Jones. I need to eat and I need to sleep. Then I need to check out this Fuchs. *Then* I'll come see you and we can talk further. If you've waited thirty years you can wait another day. And please, this time just tell me your damn jump code rather than burning it onto my retinas or something, OK?"

Jones nodded. "Twenty-four hours, Mr. Simms. I look forward to working with you again."

He began to pack up his medical instruments. Simms turned away. Once Jones had departed, Simms crossed to his window. Massive, grey clouds filled the sky, like great planetoids of stone up there. Rain smeared the hard lines of London into formless blurs. He stood and watched for a long time.

Ten hours later, Simms emerged from the Fisherman's Wharf jump node in San Francisco. As he pushed through the crowds he sent his habitual scan for shadows into the jump network. For once he saw a possible match. The probability counted up from 10% to 30% to 60%. He'd taken twelve hops to jump from London to SF, including a few through remote corners of the globe. Expensive on the private networks but it meant he was harder to follow and that any pursuer was easier to spot. The match hit 90%. Close enough. He kicked off other probes to find out more.

Snatches of hard information trickled back. He studied

it as he walked, barely seeing the streets around him. His pursuer was a man. ID encrypted, but there were other ways to identify people. The jump networks by definition knew everything about you, from your blood-group right up to what you had pierced. And what you were *thinking* of getting pierced. People forgot that, figuring they were safe by hiding the obvious information. But if you had a head full of sophisticated algorithms, the sort normally only available to the security services, you could go a long way towards piecing things together. It was a risk, opening yourself up to being spotted by the real spooks, but sometimes you had to gamble. It was just a shame actual DNA code was unobtainable. That would make life a *whole* lot easier. But the laws were insanely strict and gene sequences were encrypted so strongly as they passed through the jump networks, not even quantum computers could get at them.

Still, Simms soon retrieved enough fragmentary data to rule out anyone he knew. OK, which meant nothing. clONE, the GMA, Forty Days: any of them could pay an assassin. Something about it bugged him, though. The person was good at hiding in the data. Damn good. Had access to highly privileged encryption keys. Simms' plug-ins could identify just about anyone but *this* figure remained an unknown.

Simms hadn't had a friendly chat with Ballard recently, but the GMA tended to blunder in guns blazing. Subtlety wasn't their thing. Forty Days, perhaps? They probably had the required tech. Why would they follow him, though? They had him on a leash. clONE might be checking up on him, of course. But there was another possibility. The people who created him from Grendel's DNA. If they were still around they'd be able to afford the best. Maybe they'd heard about his investigations and come looking for him.

Just what he needed. Another bunch of maniacs on his trail.

Still weighing up the probabilities, he reached the Double Helix and pushed open the door.

He caught the brief moment of hush as he entered. He knew what it meant. It was the reaction strangers got when they blundered inside. Unwelcome strangers. Word had got round.

He ignored it and walked up to the bar. Mac stood there ready to serve, drying glasses on a white cloth. There were machines to do that, of course, but Mac preferred the manual approach. It was part of the role he liked to play. *Grizzled barman who knows everything.* Saying nothing, he poured a shot of Simms' favourite Scotch.

Simms sat on a stool at the bar and sipped at the smooth liquid, relishing its fire. "I'm looking for someone."

Mac shrugged. "Who isn't?"

"You know what I mean."

"You're right. I do." A look of hostility flashed across Mac's eyes.

"I just need the name of a genehunter, that's all," said Simms. "Doesn't matter who. Someone who specialises in the dark arts." All genehunters protected their privacy. Those who hunted the dictators and war-criminals of history, even more so. They generally weren't fun-loving party animals.

"So it's true. You are hunting genehunters now," said Mac.

"You know, I don't know why Ballard bothers with all those investigations and stings. He should just come here and ask you."

"Believe me, he does. I don't tell him anything, either."

"OK, look. I'm not hunting genehunters. Unless you mean *myself*. I'm trying to find out about my own origins, that's all. I presume you heard about that, too?"

"Some."

"What you heard is true. Someone cloned me and I don't know who or why. And a genehunter who spends their days tracking down the maniacs of history might be able to help me."

"And clONE would like to speak to them too, no doubt?"

Simms threw back the rest of his Scotch. Mac busied himself behind his bar, fussing over his glasses, like the two of them weren't even talking. The background hum of conversation had resumed but Simms knew everyone in there was waiting to see what happened.

"Maybe. But I'm not working for clONE. I give you my word. I have spoken to them, yes. They damn well took me prisoner. I had to talk my way out somehow."

Mac frowned but didn't reply.

"Come on," said Simms. "I've been coming here twenty years. You know you can trust me. I need to speak to a genehunter who might know about Grendel. That's all."

Mac placed the glass he was drying down on the bar and looked directly at Simms.

"I'll give you one name. A hunter called Eckhart. She might be able to help. She's good."

"Don't know her."

"Exactly. I'll tell her you're looking for her, give her your ping address, but that's as far as it goes. Understood? If she chooses not to talk to you, that's an end to it."

"I understand." Simms sent over the money for the drink then rose to leave, ignoring everyone sitting in the shadows. He could feel their gazes on his back.

"And Simms?" Mac called after him.

"Yeah?"

"Best you don't come back here, OK?"

Simms nodded without looking back and left.

He materialised back in London. He resisted the urge to fire off data searches on Eckhart. It would only make her suspicious. Mac would pass on the message. It was a long-shot anyway. Most likely she'd know nothing about Fuchs, who would be retired or dead by now. And he had no way of knowing whether Fuchs could even get him anywhere. Just because the old genehunter supplied the Grendel DNA to Forty Days didn't mean he'd supplied it to anyone else. There might be no connection at all. Except that all genehunters guarded the code they tracked down jealously, maintaining its scarcity value. Hoping for the happy day when they got a big pay-off for DNA they already owned. Grendel was rare, a few simple network trawls had shown that. It was at least possible Fuchs had monopolised that particular commodity.

Simms reached the safety and comfort of his stackroom without anything bad happening. Devi pinged him as he closed the door. Probably getting in touch to gloat. He thought about refusing the connection. But he needed all the help he could get. Needed to speak to someone. And there was only Devi.

"Simms. Nice exit from the Double Helix. Very dignified."

"You were there?"

"Saw it second-hand. Lots of chatter about you."

"Good chatter?"

"You know how it is. If Mac doesn't trust you, no one does."

"You're still talking to me."

"Don't want to miss the next instalment of your self-destruction. It's too entertaining."

"Glad you think so."

"So you were asking questions about a genehunter?"

"Old school guy called Fuchs."

"So you have turned gamekeeper now?"

She sounded delighted by the prospect. It was all this big joke for her. He couldn't keep the anger from his thoughts as he replied. "I don't know what the hell I am any more, do I? Everything I thought I knew is a lie. My loving parents didn't die in a car crash when I was three. Because I didn't have any damn parents. Someone set me up, set my whole life up, and I'm going to find who and why. This has nothing to do with clONE. I'm looking after myself for once."

"For once? Right. And the other thing they're saying? About Grendel. Is that true?"

"It might be."

"This gets better and better. And you think this Fuchs was involved?"

"It's a long shot. Feel free to pitch in with any other suggestions."

"I told you already, I've got nothing on Grendel. And here's the thing, if I start helping you, word will get round and I'll end up banned from the Helix, too. That would never do. Much as I long to have your body back in my bed, the fact is you're bad for business."

"I can pay. For information, I mean. Does that change how you feel? Come on, you're involved in *everything*." As he said that a thought struck him. It made sense. "Besides, you owe me here."

"I do?"

"You do. Because you sold my DNA to Forty Days in the first place. You played your part in setting all this up."

"They told you that?"

"They did. And they don't lie, as they insist on saying. I hope you got a good price for me."

Devi said nothing for moment, debating whether she believed him, maybe.

"The money was OK," she replied eventually. "Nothing special."

"Thanks. So, given how racked with guilt you must be, are you going to help me?"

Another pause. "I'll think about it."

"I thought you liked to live dangerously?"

"Sure. But mainly I like to *live*, Simms. I'll be in touch. Maybe." She cut the channel.

"Bye," said Simms into the dead connection. He kicked his way through the clutter on the floor into his kitchen.

When his espresso machine had finished roaring and steaming, he sat back on his sofa and sipped the rich, bitter liquid. He still had plenty of time before he had to meet Jones. He couldn't just sit around doing nothing. Mac or Devi might turn something up. But they might not. He might never hear from either again. If he wanted to track down the source of the Grendel DNA he had to do it himself. Thirty years ago Fuchs had done just that. Hunting down a dead madman like Grendel couldn't be that different from hunting down a dead pop star. Could it?

OK. So three decades back, either a clone of Grendel was alive or Fuchs had found a reliable tissue sample. Simms kicked off net searches for any possible sightings or leads. Chances were he'd turn up nothing. Grendel was famously paranoid and secretive, had lived his life against a storm of death-threats because of his controversial medical researches. More than one genehunter had tried and failed to acquire him. The irony was, of course, that Simms already had the man's DNA. Had *plenty* of it. What he didn't know was who had it thirty years ago.

He decided to follow the only lead he had. The one person he'd met who knew about Grendel's history. He'd promised not to visit her again, but he could probably work around that. Everyone had their price.

Ten minutes later, brain buzzing pleasantly with real caffeine molecules, he shut his stackroom door behind him. No one waited in the shadows to rearrange the layout of his internal organs. That was always good. The scuffed old hallway was as bare and empty as ever. Maybe he wasn't being followed. Or maybe they knew where he lived now and were biding their time. Whoever *they* were. He picked his way down the stairs, wary as he passed the door on each floor. He saw no one, heard nothing, except for the occasional raging argument and blare of music from the other stackrooms.

He felt safer outside, on the streets. Which was old-fashioned thinking. People would not rush to his aid if he was attacked. He got that. He wouldn't himself. If you saw trouble you kept your gaze down, hurried on. That was what you did.

He reached Euston jump station without being accosted. He picked a node in the twelve-by-twelve array for the short hop out to the suburbs of London and stepped inside.

✕✕

"Mrs. Douglas? May I have a word? Please?"

As expected he got no reply. Perhaps she'd moved on. Actually or metaphorically. Simms thought about asking the neighbours but decided against it. Last time, most of them hadn't known the old woman was even there.

"Mrs. Douglas?"

He heard movement then, feet scuffing across a bare floor. They didn't come any nearer. There was always a chance she was contacting the police. But he doubted it. How did you even do that without plug-ins? He couldn't remember, now.

"Mrs. Douglas, I hope you can hear me." He felt ridiculous shouting at a closed door. But battering it down wasn't going to help. 'last time I was here you gave me a picture. I've come back to return the favour. To give you a picture. I'm sliding it under the door now."

He stooped and pushed the image he'd printed inside.

"Her name is Eloise, Mrs. Douglas. She's my daughter. I only just met her, but I'm hoping to see her again. She's my daughter which means she's your aunt, more or less. Your Aunt Eloise."

He stood waiting, ear pressed to the flaking wood of the door. After a moment he heard gentle footsteps shuffling their way towards him. The corner of the picture sticking out beneath the door disappeared.

"She lives with her mother, a woman called Kelly. I might be wrong, but I think the three of us are the only family you have left alive."

Another pause, then the door opened slowly, the flimsy chain in place. Mrs. Douglas peered out. She looked thinner than he remembered.

"What do you want from me?" she asked.

"Thanks to your picture I know who I am, now," said Simms. "Where I come from, I mean. I really had no idea, believe me. I have all these memories of my early life. My parents, my friends, the games we played and the school I went to. Only now I know none of it was real. Someone *made* me. I was hoping you'd help me find out who."

"You're still a genehunter. You're still *him*. I know what you're capable of."

"Everything you say is true. I am a genehunter. And I was cloned from your grandfather. But that means, although you might not like the fact, you are effectively my granddaughter. I promise you I mean you no harm. I'm just looking for some answers. Please? Can I come in?"

They stood there, the two of them, for long moments, separated by the thin wood of the door. Then the chain rattled and the door was pulled open.

"Come in," she said. "But any trouble and I'll knock your fucking head off with my walking-stick. Understand?"

Ten minutes later they sat in her kitchen, leafing through the family photograph album. Simms had expected to find a hovel teeming with cats and cockroaches. But her house was pristine, everything in its place. Sunlight flooded the airy room.

He sipped the tea she'd made for him. He couldn't remember when he'd last drunk tea. He turned a page and examined a shot of Grendel, peering into a microscope in some lab.

"Mrs. Douglas, do you have anything of his I could get a DNA sample from?"

The woman tensed visibly, clutching the head of her walking-stick with her bony knuckles.

"You said you weren't here as a genehunter."

"I'm not. I hardly need his DNA. I just want to be sure I'm a match."

"You are, trust me."

"Still, I need to be sure. If there was a way?"

The woman studied him for a moment, then turned back two pages in the album. There was Grendel as a sombre-looking boy, dressed in an uncomfortable-looking suit and tie for some formal family portrait. Mrs. Douglas fished behind the photo and pulled out a plastic bag containing some curls of fair hair.

"Can you get a sequence from this?"

"Maybe from the follicles."

Simms pulled on a pair of plaskin gloves. Contamination here was *really* not going to help. With sterile tweezers he picked out a couple of likely-looking strands and dropped them into his sequencer. The device took only a few moments to confirm the match.

He wondered if she knew just how valuable the lock of hair would be to the right people. Extremely rare, provenance hard to dispute. "Thank you," he said. "Has anyone else ever extracted DNA from this?"

"No. Never shown it to anyone."

"Someone had his code thirty years ago. They must have got it from somewhere."

"Thirty years?"

"That's how old I am."

"Really? You look older. But actually, now I think about it, there was someone who came asking questions once. Years ago. Might have been about then."

"A genehunter?"

"I suppose. I didn't stop to chat."

"Did they give you their name?"

"No. People tend not to when you're chasing after them with a kitchen knife. In my experience."

"And they didn't come back?"

"Oh, no." She poured him another cup of tea from her china teapot. Who had china teapots any more?

"Maybe they did when you weren't in?"

"But I'm always in. I don't like to leave the house. Some friends bring me everything I need."

"OK, so maybe when you were asleep? They could have broken in, found this hair."

"I don't think so. I didn't see any sign of it."

"If they were good enough, you wouldn't."

Mrs. Douglas looked thoughtful for a moment. "There was one strange thing, though."

"Go on."

"I had a dog. A timid little thing. Kept me company. He disappeared about then. I woke up one morning and he'd gone. I assumed he'd got out and run away. Haven't had a pet since."

"Would it have attacked an intruder?"

"I doubt it. Hidden in a corner quivering, more likely. But I suppose an intruder wouldn't know that."

"Can you think of any other way your grandfather's DNA could have been acquired?"

"No. He was paranoid, you see. Controlling. He made very sure any tissue samples or... other sources of DNA were destroyed."

"You mean the clones he made?"

"His *simulacra*, yes. Once he'd learned what he could from them, how they developed and so forth, he destroyed them. They were experiments he was no longer interested in. And he specified the same for himself when he went."

Simms looked down at the curls of hair in his analyser. So, in all likelihood, *this* was what he came from. His whole existence from this? It wasn't much. He should be grateful to the old woman, he supposed. If it wasn't for her and this family keepsake he would never have existed.

"When I first knocked on your door," he said, "you told me to go away and that *you'd told me before*. What did you mean by that, Mrs. Douglas?"

The old woman sighed. She looked out of her window for a moment.

"There is another clone," she said eventually. "He came here ten years ago. I assumed he'd escaped from prison and come to seek his revenge. When I saw you on my doorstep I was terrified."

"From prison?"

"The human zoo he'd been kept in. Isn't that what these DNA collectors do?"

"Some."

"So, this man must have escaped and come looking for me. Looking for answers. Fortunately the friends I mentioned were able to help."

"What did they do?"

"Between us we gave him the answers he needed. Then they found him a safe place to live where he couldn't be found."

"These friends of yours. You mean clONE, right?"

"That's what they call themselves now. They're good people. They look after me even though they have no real reason to."

Which meant it most likely *was* clONE following him, hoping he'd lead them to another zoo. And what the old woman had said also meant he had a genetic twin somewhere in a refuge. Arizona? Perhaps he'd been there all along, he and the Tom Jacks clone, sitting and laughing at all Simms' difficulties.

"And before all that. Thirty years ago. Did you tell your friends what happened then?"

"I did. That's how you ended up being rescued, you see. That's why you haven't lived your entire life locked up like an exhibit in a freak show. I'm glad I did it, now."

There was a silence. Simms looked at her. She returned his gaze then turned away.

"Then you do know about my past," said Simms. "Tell me, Mrs. Douglas. Tell me everything you know. Please."

She sighed. "I really don't know much. They gave me a few details. They found you when you were two or three, so you won't remember it. They freed several people from illegal imprisonment. As a group you were referred to as *sims*, just because it's short for *simulacra* I suppose. You'd got it into your head that was your name. They tried to call you something else, a proper name, but you were having none of it."

Simms nodded. He'd always been Simms. He'd never really thought about why. "But my memories. My parents. Our house in the suburbs. The family dog."

"Oh, that was all real. They found you foster parents. A fresh start with a loving family. But then I believe there was a car accident and you lost them both? Terrible. After that, from what I know, you moved around a lot, were never really settled."

"I remember them. I was happy there, although I didn't realise it until afterwards. I thought perhaps it was all a lie, false memories implanted into my brain."

"Oh, no. It was all real."

Simms nodded. It felt good to know that. Some small part of himself he could believe in. He tried to make sense of it all, of who he was. It was too much. Understanding it would take time. All he could do for now was focus on the job, the immediate problem. This collector had owned at least two separate zoos. Was there a third? Did he have another genetic twin imprisoned somewhere? They'd still have the DNA. It had to be likely. He just had to find out who and where they were.

"Can you tell me anything else that might be of use? About those who created me?"

"I'm afraid not. clONE didn't know much themselves. They found the collection but not the people who owned it. The people responsible."

Simms nodded. It was always the way.

"Would you like another cup of tea?" the woman asked.

"No. I have to go. Someone I need to see. But you've given me a lot to think about. I'm grateful."

"I'm sorry I can't help you more."

"You've been extremely helpful, Mrs. Douglas."

"You must come again. I'm always here."

"I thought you preferred your own company?"

"I do. But, well, you're close enough, aren't you?"

"I'll try, when all this is over. I promise."

"Good. And make sure you don't lose Kelly and Eloise. Living alone can get very tiresome, believe me."

Simms nodded. "I'll do what I can."

✕

This time when he climbed the stairs to his stackroom someone *was* there, waiting for him. Outside, at least, so not Gideon Jones. His shadow in the jump network? Could be. Whoever it was made no attempt to conceal themselves. Just leaned against the wall awaiting his return. His room's systems picked up weapons: a couple of blasters and three concealed blades. But you couldn't criticise someone for a little thing like that.

Maybe it was a clever ambush. Maybe it was just someone wanting to say *hi*. Warily, he walked to meet them.

"Waiting for me?" he asked.

"Obviously."

A woman's voice, not one he knew. Nothing from her plug-ins. Inevitably. She stepped forward, out of the shadows. She had short, severe hair and a short, severe look on her face. Her clothes were deliberately drab. She could only be Eckhart. Simms had never seen her before: not on a job, not even in the Double Helix. Which maybe just showed how good she was. So why was she here now? A strange time to reveal herself, especially with all the chatter about him.

"Mac sent you?"

"Mac told me about you."

"Should I invite you in or are you planning to blow my head off with those blasters?"

"You should invite me in. I'll let you know on the blaster thing."

"How did you find me?"

The woman shrugged. "You weren't hard to track down."

Maybe she was the one following him through the jump network. Except, he'd first picked up the shadow on the way to the Double Helix hadn't he? Still. It didn't matter. She was here now. Simms instructed his security to deactivate and showed her inside.

Inside, she stood in the middle of the room, assessing. It was exactly what he'd do in a hostile situation.

"I got coffee and I got Scotch," said Simms. "Or, if you like, I can do coffee *and* Scotch."

"No. You wanted to see me?"

Simms sat, letting her look down on him. Maybe it would put her at ease a little. "I'm trying to find out about a hunter called Fuchs. He tracked down the code of Dr. Grendel, thirty years ago. I'd like to find out more about him."

"Fuchs is long dead."

"You knew him?"

"I knew someone who did. They're dead, too."

"You must have something, otherwise you wouldn't be here."

"A little. Fuchs kept good records. When he died the hunter I knew inherited them."

Or, more likely, Fuchs had been killed for the information he had. That was encouraging. "Right. And when this other hunter so sadly died, you were next in line?"

"Yeah."

"And what information have you got?"

"That depends, doesn't it?"

"Let me tell you what I know," said Simms. "Thirty years ago, this Fuchs broke into the house of Dr. Grendel's granddaughter and retrieved a DNA sample without her knowledge. He handed this sample over to his client. It was viable and at least one clone was produced. In all likelihood, Fuchs also sold the code to Forty Days when they came looking for it."

Eckhart shrugged. "If you know so much what do you need from me?"

"The client. I need to know who that was. Did Fuchs' records say?"

"There are some details."

"Enough to track them down?"

"If you know what you're doing."

"OK, Eckhart. Assuming I do know what I'm doing, are you willing to provide me those details? I can, of course, pay."

"I know you can pay. But I'm not sure you'll like my price."

"Tell me how much you want. I'm real good with numbers."

"Well, here's the thing. I could name a fee and you'd pay me and we'd both be happy. But you have something more valuable. Something that will continue to pay in years to come."

What the hell did she mean? Then he saw it. That was why she was here in person.

"So Grendel's code wasn't in Fuchs' records."

"That's correct."

"And you thought you could come here, take a sample of my DNA and spend the rest of your days selling copies of it to the highest bidder?"

"Something like that."

"You really think I'd do that?"

"I think you might. Depends how much you want what I've got."

The thought of it disgusted him. Like he'd be giving

himself away, selling himself. Yet it was only something he'd done countless times before. When it wasn't his DNA.

"How do you know I am his clone?"

"I don't. I've heard all the stories about you, but stories don't mean anything. Fortunately, Fuchs' records did contain a checksum calculated from Grendel's code. I'll know if you're him."

The muscles in Simms' face clenched. She saw it and tensed, preparing for his attack. Had she said that to goad him? Probably not. Just a turn of phrase. Still, he should blast her fucking head off. He was Simms, not Grendel.

Instead he looked away, out of his window, willing himself to stay calm. He had no real choice. He never had a choice. He had to find out. And that meant he needed to trade with Eckhart.

"What do you have?" he asked. "Names? IDs?"

"The client insisted on meeting Fuchs face-to-face. Said they could judge him better by looking him in the eye."

"So you have video?"

"Single frames. But the face is very clear."

"Show me."

Eckhart shook her head. "Blood first. If you check out you can have the pictures."

"And if you've faked them just to get my DNA?"

"Then you're screwed. That's the chance you have to take."

She was treating him like a civilian, a mere client, not a fellow genehunter. Genehunters fought and killed each other if they were working the same job, sure, but they trusted each other when it came to trading. That was the code. You lived by your reputation.

He stood abruptly, enjoying seeing her flinch. He held out his arm to her. "OK. Take what you came for, Eckhart."

Eckhart pulled a med-kit from her pocket, keeping her eyes on him all the time. At least there were no scalpels in this one.

"Roll up your sleeve," she said.

She worked the crook of his elbow looking for a vein, found one she liked. "I'm afraid this will hurt a little."

She slid the slanting tip of the syringe into him. He refused to wince or react in any way. Dark blood began to flow. When she had enough, she pulled the syringe out and covered his wound with a swab. "Press here until it stops bleeding."

"Yeah. I know how it works. So tell me, you got a match?"

A moment's pause. "I got it. Congratulations. You must be very proud."

"Now send me the pictures."

She hesitated for a moment, enjoying her moment of power over him.

"Sure. Here they are."

The images arrived in Simms' head, five still shots of a young-looking woman looking directly face-on, mid-conversation. He didn't need to run any facial-recognition scans to identify her. Memories from the Tom Jacks case flashed through his mind. The collector. The woman Mann had been working for. He'd met her and hadn't known.

"If you're good enough you might be able to track her down," said Eckhart.

Simms focused back on Eckhart. "Oh, but I already know who she is. Thank you, Eckhart, you've been very helpful. Now fuck off out of my life and don't ever come back."

Eckhart shrugged, turned away. At the door she paused. "Just make sure you stay out of my life, too. OK, Simms? You and clONE."

When she'd gone he stood at his window. After a minute or two he saw her down on the ground, an ant crawling away from the foot of his stacktower.

He thought about what he should do. He still had ten

hours before his rendezvous with Jones. He should probably get some sleep. No telling what Forty Days had in store for him. Only, he wasn't tired. He buzzed with anticipation. Eckhart had taken him straight to the people responsible for cloning him. He had enough time to make his first move there, set himself up with them. It was a gamble. But either he'd get somewhere and be out in time to see Jones. Or it would all go wildly wrong, in which case his problems with Forty Days would be irrelevant.

He set off for Euston jump node again. As he walked he worked out how he was going to play it. He made two calls. One to Mann, requesting a meeting. The other to a woman in Arizona he really needed to get a message through to first.

✕

"Mr. Simms. What an unexpected pleasure."

Five hours later, Simms was finally admitted into Mann's wood-panelled office. Everything just as he'd seen it during the Tom Jacks case.

"Good of you to see me," said Simms. "I'm sure you're a busy man."

"Alas, so. Now, how exactly may I help? I believe the normal arrangement is for paying client to contact genehunter, rather than *vice versa?*"

There was a good chance Mann didn't know anything. Almost certainly wouldn't have been here thirty years ago. Simms had to get past him to his employer, the woman he'd met on his previous visit. The collector.

"I'm here to check you were happy with my service," said Simms. "Customer satisfaction is very important to me. Also, it occurred to me I had access to several other genomes your employer might be interested in."

"You wish to see my employer?"

"Not necessarily now, obviously. At some convenient time. If she's interested." It sounded weak even as he said it.

"Hmm." Mann paused to think. Or, more likely, to communicate with the woman who paid for his comfortable lifestyle. Of course, she'd know who Simms was. Genetically. She must have known when they first met. She might even have guessed he'd been the one in her collection all those years ago. She'd be suspicious, now. Question was, would she take the bait or refuse to see him?

"Perhaps I should call back," said Simms. "At a more convenient time. Please, if you ever need the services of a genehunter, you know how to reach me." He rose to leave.

Mann watched him but made no attempt to stop him. "Very well, Mr. Simms. As you say, we know very well how to reach you."

Simms stepped into the private jump node.

He emerged in a plain, square room, just him and the bare walls and the metal frame of the jump node. Wherever he was, it wasn't Euston. They'd taken the bait.

Immediately, he sent a probe back into the gate to retrieve the address he'd been rerouted to. It was a matter of some importance. If it differed from the one he'd retrieved on his last visit to Mann's office, he would never see the light of day again. It was as simple as that.

"So, Simms, you've finally come home. How touching. And, my, haven't you grown?"

Bright lights flooded the room, blinding him for a moment. Mann's employer stood in the doorway. No, stood *outside* the doorway. Clearly there was a force-wall protecting her. The trap had been sprung. Question was, who had fallen into whose trap?

She looked no different from before, the same young body and old eyes. If he had to guess, he'd say she was somewhere between twenty and one hundred and fifty. Something like that.

"So you do recognize me?" he said.

"Of course. Our first Grendel clone, back where he

belongs. The prodigal son returning. Now, I'd be grateful if you could remove all your weapons. Obviously there's no point trying to conceal any. Also, you'll find your plug-ins are suppressed. We'll keep them that way until we have time to cut them from your brain."

He ran diagnostics on his hardware, alarm fluttering in his chest. She was right. All offline. Not good. No way of knowing, now, whether he was in the right place or not. One by one he let his blasters and knives and wires and microbombs fall to the floor.

"Did you know who I was when you first contacted me?"

"As a matter of fact, no. That was quite the surprise. Then I realised you must be my original clone, all grown up. I'd assumed you'd died years ago."

He dropped his last blade and held his arms wide. No one emerged from the jump node behind him to save him. He needed to keep her talking. If they sent him on to some other zoo he'd be lost.

"You've been shadowing me through the jump networks?"

"No. We hired someone to find out about you. Tell us your secrets. So much easier."

"Who?"

"I suppose it hardly matters now. A genehunter called Devi. She said you knew her?"

Jesus Christ. You couldn't trust anyone. Still he had to hand it to Devi, she'd played it nicely. Damn her. "Yeah, I may have come across her. But I'm confused. When you found out about me, you did nothing. Left me to run around in freedom. Why?"

"Oh, you had so little idea who you were and what was going on. Endearing, really. I decided you were more use than threat. You *are* a very good genehunter. But coming here changes everything. If I leave you at liberty you're a liability. Here, you're an asset. A valuable asset."

"I'll be missed by people."

"Will you? I doubt it. They'll shrug and move on. Say *you had it coming* and forget about you."

"You're going to keep me here?"

"Or trade you. You're very valuable. Our other Grendel clone is much younger. You look so much more like the real thing."

"So you do have another. I'm surprised. You seem to keep losing us."

"I do?"

"Me thirty years ago. The other ten years back."

"Technically he wasn't ours. He escaped during a trade to another collector. Now, would you like a look around? Meet all your new friends?" She cancelled the force-wall with a sweep of her hand. "Obviously there is no point trying to attack me. You'd be incapacitated before you could get close."

"Obviously."

He walked into a brightly lit corridor. It led to a cavernous room, artificially lit, no doors or windows. It could be anywhere. Deep underground, beneath the ocean, on the damn moon. Filling it were around thirty circular habitats, each about the size of his stackroom. An igloo and a little patch of garden. Each isolated and highly secure, surrounded by an outer dome of inch-thick mesh. A grim place to spend a lifetime. Weirdly, a carpeted trail led amongst them. How many of the woman's rich friends and fellow collectors had come down here to stare at all the ruthless murderers and tyrants?

They walked around the edge of the first compound. A man he vaguely recognized sat on a chair in his little garden, watching them. He looked old and tired, his straight black hair turning to grey. Simms accessed his plug-in to help him ID the man, but obviously he got nothing. Something to do with the Second World War? He should have paid more attention in his history lessons.

They walked on, past a chubby-faced Asian youth and a frowning older man with a bushy beard. Both regarded

Simms and the woman with an undisguised hate. No one spoke.

"So, I've been here before?" asked Simms. "This is where I was born?"

The woman stopped and turned to study him. "Ah, so that's it. You came here to find out about your past. A poor lost boy all alone in the world, confused about who you are. You weren't hoping to acquire DNA or get your revenge, were you? You just came in a sad little attempt to find out about yourself."

"I know who I am. Just tell me the facts."

She shrugged. "There's nothing to tell. What were you hoping for, Simms? Some fairy-story of loving parents? Yes, you were born here. Bred from the DNA of Dr. Grendel to fill a hole in my collection. That's all you are. All you ever were. And now you're back where you belong."

"You make me sick," he said. "You're not human."

"But we're all humans," she said. "At least I know what sort of person I am. You don't seem to have a clue."

She set off again. He had no choice but to follow her. If he refused she'd have a way of coercing him. Why had he come here? What had he been hoping to find out? He'd wanted to see for himself, sure, but it was always obvious what he would discover.

The woman stopped at another habitat. "Now here's someone you will want to meet." She sounded delighted at the prospect. "I'll put you in the house next door so you can get to know each other. Although I suppose you already do."

She pressed a button and a bell sounded inside the little house. After a moment, the door was pushed open and a man shuffled out, obeying his summons. He was maybe twenty years old but his face was completely familiar. He stopped when he saw Simms.

"We just call him Grendel," said the woman. "He was born here, like you. From the same code."

The man, Simms' genetic twin, strode forwards to the mesh. Without speaking he spat in Simms face.

"Oh dear," said the woman. "I'm afraid they all know who you are and what you do. You won't be the most popular person in here. Although, if I'm honest, they all hate each other. They're such children."

Simms wiped his face. He wanted to say something to his clone. Apologize, maybe. He couldn't find the words. He wasn't responsible for this place, but there were other collections he had helped fill. This was what he'd done with his life. He was no better then the original Grendel. Worse, really.

"Now," said the woman. "Over here is your new home. It's bare but comfortable. Obviously you can't escape, although I'm sure you'll try. You are free to do as you wish except when we have visitors. Then I expect you to make an appearance, answer their questions, do as they ask."

"And if I refuse?"

"I really suggest you don't. There are various punishments that can be rather unpleasant. Judging by the screams, anyway."

She showed him in and locked the gate behind him. She reached through the mesh to stroke his face. "So lovely to have you back home, little boy," she said. Then she turned and walked away.

Simms sat on the floor inside, in the darkness, and put his head in his hands. This was not what he'd planned. No one was coming to rescue him. This was going to be his life from now on. He'd faced death many times and had always wriggled his way out. Now he wished he hadn't. A quick end would have been preferable. Devi must have told them of his connection to clONE. Told them everything. So he'd been caught in the collector's trap after all. Maybe it wasn't even *for* him. Maybe he was just the bait to draw out clONE, exact revenge for thirty years earlier.

He shook his head in the dark. If, somehow, he did see Devi again, he'd have to congratulate her. Right before reducing her body to fucking atoms. And what would Kelly think of him? That he'd changed identities and run away. She'd think until the day the bombs started falling and the world ended. There was only one bright spot in the whole mess. He was safe from Jones and Ballard. He was safe from everyone, now.

He must have fallen asleep, then. He slipped in and out of confused dreams in which Jones and Ballard and Kelly and Devi and Nemesis were all in his head, all shouting instructions at him. But they all screamed over the top of each other, so he couldn't make out what any of them wanted.

He jerked awake, heart thudding. Booming explosions echoed through the air. The ground shook with repeated concussions. He stood and ran to the door. Black smoke roiled through the great vault, lit by red flash after red flash. He heard shouting, gunfire, impossible to say from where. Heavily armed guards ran in the direction of the jump node, firing off blaster bursts as they went.

Simms darted into his little garden. Maybe the security systems had been knocked out and he could sneak away unseen. An explosion nearby buffeted against his face. He pushed at the security gate. It swung open. He strode outside, trying to get his bearings in the thick air. Indistinct figures ran past him, impossible to say whether they were guards or prisoners.

He was about to sprint for the jump node when a blaster shot cut through the rolling smoke and into his head, sending him reeling to the floor.

He came round with the soft carpet of the walkway against his face, the dusty taste of it in his mouth. His head throbbed with heavy pain. He reached up to touch the side of his head, expecting to find some deep hole. He felt the warm wetness of blood, but no deep wound. A glancing blow. Squinting through the smoke and pain, Simms looked up and around. The battle still raged. More explosions boomed through the air, punctuated by lines of blaster fire. Without armour or a gun of his own, he had no damn chance. On hands and knees, he crawled back inside his little house to sit the battle out.

He lay face down on the floor, arms over his head, until the fighting began to die down. Still he didn't move. Things could kick off again at any moment. What the hell was going on out there? Who had won? Come to that, who was even *fighting*?

He heard the click of his door being pushed open. Looking up he could see a figure dressed in full combat armour, holding a blaster rifle. Simms stood on wobbly legs to face them, not knowing who or what to expect. The visitor pulled up their visor so he could see who it was.

"Nemesis. You took your time getting here."

The woman slung her blaster across her back. "Took us time to hack through their security."

"The address I sent was right?"

"It was. How did you get it?"

"Probably best you don't know." Probably best he didn't say he'd been selling the illegally-acquired DNA of Tom Jacks. "Did you catch her? The collector?"

The woman he knew only as Nemesis smiled. The first time he'd seen her smile. "We got her. Finally. Alive and kicking. Literally."

"What happens to her now?"

"We pass her to the GMA."

"Be sure to tell Agent Ballard how useful I was."

"I will."

"And the clones?"

"We'll triage them. Offer them a refuge. But it's up to them. They're free to do as they please. None of them has done anything wrong."

"And what about me? Are you planning on offering me a new home, too?"

"We are grateful to you, Simms."

"What does that mean?"

She considered for a moment. "It means yes. You'd be monitored, of course. On probation. This could all be some elaborate scheme to gain access to the people we look after. But yes, you've made the first step."

"And Kelly?"

"That's up to her, isn't it? Come on, let's get you out of here."

Nemesis turned and held open the door. Outside, the smoke was beginning to clear. A squad of clONE soldiers stood there, weapons at the ready. All around, inmates were being helped from their houses. Some refused to go, struggling and screaming. They'd known nothing else their entire lives. What could you do, *make* them free? Others filed off looking dazed or wary. Simms caught the eye of his twin. There may have been the briefest nod. Then Grendel turned and walked away.

"You should come to the refuge so we can check you out," said Nemesis. "You're hurt."

His mind finally began to work properly. "Wait. How long have I been in here?"

"Five hours or so."

Five hours. His deadline with Jones must be about up. His plug-ins were still offline so he couldn't tell for sure.

"The time, Nemesis. What's the time?"

She told him. He had minutes to spare.

"Sorry, but I have to be somewhere else."

Nemesis raised an eyebrow but didn't reply.

"I can just leave?" said Simms.

"The jump node is open. You know where we are if

you need us."

Simms raced off. A thought hit him and he turned back. "Nemesis. Have you been shadowing me? Through the jump networks?"

"No," she said. "Why? Should we have?"

Simms grinned and raced for the node.

☒

"Well, well, Mr. Simms. So you decided to join us after all."

"I said I'd come. I don't lie, either."

Simms stood in a high, shadowy room at the end of Jones' jump address. It resembled the church in Sienna more than anything: a tall, airy, vaulted space, echoing with footsteps. Although the church hadn't had blaster-clusters arrayed around its walls. The room was windowless and clearly modern, its stones fresh-cut and clean. Jones stood in front of a phalanx of tall soldiers, each holding a spear-length version of the Forty Days sharpened crucifix.

"Of course," said Jones. "How could I have doubted you? Are you injured?"

"It's nothing. What do you want? What's this job of yours?"

Jones regarded him for a moment longer, like he hadn't finally decided about him. Finally he spoke.

"Do you remember what I said to you the first time we met? My message?"

"Sure. *The Soldiers of Megiddo gather.*"

"And do you understand what I meant?"

Simms shrugged. "I guess."

"The end times are approaching, Mr. Simms. The final days. The last battle between good and evil."

"Uh huh."

"You see, you and I, we're both soldiers in that army." Jones' face lit up now, his usual bland expression replaced by a look of rapture. Simms had to suppress a yawn. The blood trickling down the side of his head tickled his neck. "But we're just foot-soldiers, aren't we?" Jones continued. "Cannon-fodder. I've invited you here to show you the Generals in the army. The ones who will lead us to victory. Follow me into the *Sanctum Sanctorum*."

Jones turned and left. The stone-faced guards stood unmoving, watching Simms. Simms followed Jones as instructed and the guards moved with him, surrounding him. They passed through three arched doorways, each higher and more ornate that the last. He still had no clue where he was. His plug-ins were back online, but they could get no geographic fix on his location.

Finally, they entered a vast hallway, tall pillars reaching up to a high, vaulted roof. A modern-day cathedral. In the centre stood a wide, circular dais, floored with marble and edged with gold. Set upon it, like the markings on a giant clock, stood twelve sarcophagi. No, not sarcophagi. They were machines, blinking with lights and readouts. Simms knew, then, what they were. Cloning vats. Eleven were occupied. One was dark. Which was presumably where he came in.

A man knelt in the middle of the circles, dressed in the sort of flowing robes that priests always seemed to wear. At first Simms thought the man was ill, slumped there on his knees, but then he understood. He was praying. At Jones' approach, the man rose to his feet, one hand on his spear-length crucifix. He looked tall, an effect accentuated by the absurd clerical hat he wore. It offered no defensive qualities at all that Simms could see.

The man's gaze was fixed on Simms, a look of distaste clear on his face. Jones approached the man, dipping his head in supplication. Whoever this was, he outranked Jones. Standing close, the two conversed, although whether in whispers or electronically, Simms couldn't tell. That was fine. He had no intention of getting any closer.

They finished their conversation and Jones turned to face Simms. A look of triumph lit up his face. He held out his arms as if revealing the twelve vats for the first time. "Do you understand now, Mr. Simms? The glory of His great plan?"

Simms shook his head. He didn't understand at all. "This is Boneyard? This is it? To be honest I expected something more impressive."

"Oh no, Mr. Simms. *This* isn't Boneyard. Tell me, do you know why we call ourselves Forty Days?"

Simms shrugged. He knew little about such things. "Something to do with forty days in the wilderness?"

"That's what most people think. In fact, the period of forty days crops up several times in the Bible. Our name is taken from a different occurrence. The forty days of rain the Lord sent to cleanse the Earth of evil."

"Right. Noah's arc."

"Exactly. And these are the twelve who will lead the tribes in the new world that is to follow."

"The new world?"

"The new world, Mr. Simms. When our planet is once again cleansed of its sin. Cleansed of its *sinners*."

"So Boneyard..."

"Yes. You understand. *This* isn't Boneyard. Boneyard is the whole Earth. Everything out there. The world after we turn it into a killing field. The world after we unleash the one thousand nuclear warheads we have stockpiled around the world."

Jones waved a hand. Around the walls of the great room, screens began to light up: tens, hundreds of them. On each was video of a towering white missile in its silo, the name *Divine Fire* emblazoned across it. Words overlaid on each screen showed that missile's location: London, Newer York, Sydney, Beijing…

"I told you we had rich backers," said Jones. "As you can see, we have spent their money wisely. When the fires have raged and the Earth is safe once more, the select few who remain can start again. Live in peace and harmony under the wise rule of these twelve. Isn't it glorious?"

Simms looked at Jones. The guy was serious. He meant every word. For once in his life Simms couldn't think of a damn thing to say.

"So, Mr. Simms," said Jones. "Are you with us or against us?"

5 - BONEYARD

Simms half-stepped, half-fell from the gateway at London Euston jump node. He sprawled forwards onto the concrete and lay unmoving for a moment, gazing through a blurred confusion of hurrying legs. His med plug-in pumped painkillers into him but the wound in his head - the second wound in his head - throbbed sharply. Between the analgesia and all the blood he'd lost, he was finding it hard to think straight. Still, he didn't care. He'd escaped Forty Days. They were insane, utterly insane. If there was a scale, they were *way* off the end. They weren't even in sight from the end.

And he had agreed to work for them. What the hell did that make him?

Gritting his teeth, he climbed to his knees and up onto wobbly legs. Someone rushing for a gateway knocked him sideways, nearly sending him reeling to the ground. He should have stayed lying down like Jones had said. Given himself time to recover from the operation. But he hadn't wanted to remain in their damn secret lair a moment longer. He'd get home, crawl through the streets if he had to, and crash out in his own room. Where he wasn't surrounded by insane fanatics preparing to unleash a nuclear holocaust for the greater good of humanity.

He set off, lunging for the door to the street. His fellow travellers swore at him as he stumbled in their way. Perhaps they thought he was just some drugged-up loser. Perhaps they were right. The two wounds on his head, the blaster shot and the incision from Jones' trepanning saw, wouldn't be doing wonders for his appearance.

Outside, the bright sun sent more pain lancing into his skull. Why couldn't it be grey and raining today of all days? He thought about pinging someone to come help. Kelly, maybe. But his current appearance would do nothing to endear him to her. Devi? She still hadn't got back in touch. Probably wasn't going to now. Nemesis? Too many questions. He had no choice but to stagger home by himself.

It took over an hour. Three times he had to sit against a wall to stop the world spinning and tipping him off. Once he retched up bile, the taste bitter in his mouth. Fortunately no one took a knife to him to harvest his organs or brain hardware. Probably didn't look worth the effort. His plug-ins somehow kept his legs moving. And for once, miracle of miracles, the lift in his stacktower was running. He'd never seen a happier sight in his whole life than their metal doors juddering open to whisk him up forty stories.

In his room, he fell onto the bed and was immediately unconscious.

He returned to life a full day later. The world hadn't ended while he slept. That was always good. The pain in his head had subsided to a dull ache, but his mouth was parched, his tongue welded to the roof of his mouth. He felt his way to the kitchen, drank a pint of cold water, then grappled with the espresso machine, his hands shaking. It was a full ten minutes before he sat on his couch, eyes closed, sipping thick, sweet coffee.

OK, he had some thinking to do. Forty Days was going to kill everyone on the planet. Everyone apart from the twelve thousand *anointed* on their list. Once the world was cleansed of its sinners, they and the twelve cloned saints appointed to lead them would awake. The dawn of a new age of peace and harmony.

It sounded hideous. He got what they meant, sure. The world was fucked up. Life was a battle. Everyone was out to get you. Still, there had to be a better approach than killing everyone and starting again.

Except, he'd agreed to help them do just that. Agreed because he'd been offered the one thing he'd work for. His name on the list. The same for Kelly and Eloise. All he had to do was track down the DNA of a second saint and the end of the world could begin.

The problem was this: for all its nightmares, he quite liked the world as it was. The chaos and the dirt and the struggle. The fight to get to the end of the day in one piece. The unexpected flash of beauty amid the ugliness. His life wasn't perfect, not anywhere near, but it was *his* life. He'd miss it. A shot of his favourite whisky. Sparring with Devi. Mrs. Douglas and her ridiculous china teapot. Eloise. All of it.

Yet if he tried to stop Forty Days and they found out, he'd be off the list. Kelly and Eloise, too. He'd hear nothing more until the day the bombs started falling. Did he have the right to jeopardize his daughter's future like that? Probably not. But what sort of future would she have in a world bombed back to the stone age and run by religious fanatics?

He didn't know. The questions were too big. He'd do what he always did. Walk the line. Try to stop them but make sure they didn't know anything about it in case it went badly wrong. Which it most likely would.

Problem was, they'd made it *real* hard for him to do that. Another plug-in embedded in his brain. This time not hidden; he could feel it ticking away in there when he ran diagnostics. It saw everything he saw and heard everything he heard. Every ping communication. Keeping Forty Days in the dark was not going to be easy.

His only hope was the forces of law and order. This was too big for clONE; you needed a fucking army to take on Forty Days. And the only person in authority who even knew about him was his old friend, Ballard. Which meant he had to side with the GMA, temporarily at least. And it also meant that, somehow, he had to speak to Ballard without Forty Days knowing about it. How the hell was he going to pull off that trick?

Two hours later, he had a plan. It was dangerous and crazy, but he had nothing else. Getting off-network for a private chat was easy. The hard part was making it look like something else was going on. But it was this or do what Jones had told him to. And Simms didn't like to do what anyone told him to.

He began to wander around his room, picking up discarded clothes and dirty plates. Anyone monitoring the input from his optic nerves would think he was tidying. Which, if they knew him, would seem pretty unlikely, but that was the risk. He soon discovered how hard it was to find something without being able to look for it. What he needed was a piece of paper and some sort of pen. But who wrote things down any more?

Eventually he spotted an old marker in a drawer in his kitchen, once used to label tissue samples for some job. He noted its presence but ignored it. Then, coming back after a few minutes, standing with his back to the drawer, he reached inside and scrabbled around for it. When he had it he tried it out on the wall, being sure to keep it out of sight. Glancing at it a few minutes later, pretending to put some dishes down, he saw the mark he'd made. It was faint, but it would do. He slipped the pen into his back-pocket.

Now he needed paper. The photograph of Grendel.

Somewhere on his table. Maybe using that would convince Ballard he was serious. And maybe it wouldn't.

He put on some music to cover the squeaks of the marker pen. Tom Jacks seemed appropriate. Keeping the photograph well out of sight, Simms reached out with his right hand and began to write. He had to concentrate hard to resist the urge to look. If his scrawl was illegible his plan would have no chance. It was years since he'd written anything and it was possible he'd produced nothing but a scribble. It was also possible the marker had run out of ink after the first letter. He didn't dare check.

When he'd completed his message he folded the picture up three times and slipped it into his back pocket. Now to get it to Ballard. Obviously he couldn't march into a police station and hand it over. Fortunately he had a jump address. His habitual paranoia about the networks had paid off again. Just as he'd acquired the secret address of Mann's employer, he also had the address Ballard had once diverted him to: the bare cell Simms had found himself in after leaving the Bethesda Eternity Clinic. If he timed the jumps he could make it look like an accident, the briefest appearance in a nondescript white room. Forty Days might not even notice if they weren't watching at the precise moment. Another risk worth taking.

He thawed out some bread and ate eight slices of toast before heading back down to Euston. He stood in front of one of the gateways in the old six-by-six array, chosen because they still had the old manual-entry keypads. He transmitted his destination via his plug-in then, looking away, began to type in the extra address using the rusty buttons on the frame of the gateway. He had to be careful, feeling for each number before punching it in. One extra hop to Ballard's interrogation cell. A one second pause. Then on to Rome, the destination he'd originally entered. One digit wrong and he'd end up on five different continents at the same time.

When he was ready, he took out the folded photo and

held it tight in his fist. Taking a deep breath he stepped into the jump node.

He materialised in the room he remembered. That was good. Had Ballard left it open in case Simms needed to get in touch? Was Ballard that smart? Hard to say. Simms closed his eyes and tossed the folded photo into the room. A moment later, before it could even hit the floor, he felt the disorientating lurch of the next jump. When he opened his eyes again he was in the atrium of Rome Central, the air echoing with the sound of thousands of travellers striding to and from the gateways.

Now he had to hope Ballard got the message. And could read it. And believed it. And gave a damn. A lot could go wrong, a hell of a lot.

He spent an hour wandering Rome, sitting at cafés near to churches, surveying possible targets. So he hoped Forty Days would think. The remains of more than one of their saints were here in the Eternal City. Simms itched to hurry back to his stackroom, but that might look suspicious.

Eventually he could stand it no longer and jumped home to prepare for his visitor. He opened the drawer where he kept his stash of vintage acid. He took great care to let Forty Days glimpse what he was doing. Once he was ready he walked into his kitchen and poured himself more water. He stood and drank, pretending to be lost in thought. What he was actually doing was opening the concealed safe in the kitchen wall behind him. Triggering the biometric lock was tricky when you couldn't see what you were doing. He got it eventually. Reaching in, he found the disruptor ring and slipped it on his finger. He'd try not to let Forty Days see his hand, but surely they wouldn't notice a little change like that?

Then he lay back on his couch and injected the acid directly into a vein in the crook of his elbow. Again, he made a show of it, letting Forty Days see. But he left most of the liquid in the syringe and squirted it onto the floor while glancing away. He needed to take enough for the sensory disturbances to kick in, but not so much that he couldn't function when Ballard lumbered in. Assuming he was going to.

Pretty quickly the acid began to screw with him. The walls of his room pulsed and writhed while circles of bright colour flowered around him. Forty Days would obviously not approve. He had to hope they wouldn't strike him off their list there and then. He watched the show a while and waited, aiming for ten minutes but aware his judgement of time would be impaired. The images grew more disturbing and disorientating. He shut his eyes. Hopefully Forty Days would think he was about to pass out. He lifted his hand to touch his head. His skull felt distant, weird, but he was pretty sure it was his own. He pressed the ring on his finger into contact with his scalp. The small patch of shaved hair where Jones had made his incision.

Using a disruptor was highly illegal, of course. Was it illegal to use one on yourself? Maybe no one had bothered to outlaw such a thing because they figured no one would be so stupid. But that was what he was going to do. Send a strong EM pulse into his own brain to flip out his plug-ins without, hopefully, frying the tissues of his brain. He counted to three, then tapped the activation pattern onto the ring.

He experienced the briefest spike of pain in his eyeballs and, for some reason, his toes, before passing out.

He came round from the blackout feeling… weird. Disconnected, like waking up from an anaesthetic or coming round from a migraine. He checked his internal clock. Offline. Hopefully not permanently. Had he damaged brain tissues? Memory loss was a common side-effect of EM disruption. He ran through a list of names. Kelly, Devi, Ballard, Mac, Jones, recalling the face of each. OK. It seemed like he could still remember people. He opened his eyes.

He seemed to be looking at his room through the

wrong end of a telescope. Not so good. Hard to tell if it was an effect of the acid or the disruptor. Hopefully it was temporary either way. He checked through his plug-ins. All offline. No way of knowing for how long. Now he needed Ballard to show up so they could talk.

He waited ten, fifteen minutes, lying on his couch with his eyes closed and his hand over his face. He thought about risking a second disruptor shot but decided against it. Permanent brain damage didn't appeal. If he didn't already have it.

"So this is where you live? I expected something more impressive."

Simms opened an eye to see Ballard standing in his doorway, his face melted-wax once more. Maybe that made it easier to change his appearance when he needed to. His face was pretty much a blank canvass now.

"All the bribes I have to pay you," said Simms, sitting up. He had to concentrate. Play his cards correctly.

Ballard grinned. Probably. It came out more like an ugly sneer. He stepped into the room. "You look like shit."

"Great to see you, too."

"So what have you got? Are you wasting my time again or have you finally found out something about Boneyard?"

"I've found out *everything*. Now sit down and shut up while I do your damn job for you. I don't have much time."

When he'd finished his story, Ballard sat in silence for a while, considering everything Simms had said. "Why would you tell me all this?" he said at last. "Why would you want to stop Forty Days if you're on their list?"

"The thought of not seeing your smiling face again is too much to bear."

Ballard shook his head. "You're a sociopath, Simms. You don't like people and people don't like you. Killing everyone on the planet should suit you fine."

"You don't know anything about me."

"I understand you better than you understand yourself.

You're not cut out to be the good guy. You're never going to change."

"Are you prepared to give me what I want in return for Forty Days or not?"

"I don't know what you want yet."

"All investigations dropped. My records with the GMA deleted. A clean slate."

"And if I refuse?"

Simms shrugged. "Then you die. Everyone dies. Apart from the lucky few of us on the list."

"And if I lock you away you in another cell?"

"Then we'll go together when the bombs fall. How romantic."

"You wouldn't last a week in the world Forty Days want to create," said Ballard.

"Maybe. Or maybe I'd have fun converting them all to the dark side. Look, there isn't time for this. The fact you're here says you need me."

Ballard considered again. "Perhaps we can lose what we have on you. If you give us Forty Days."

"I also want all the rake-offs I've ever given you refunded. The 40K from the Tom Jacks case. All of it."

Ballard's anger was clear even through his distorted facial features. "Don't push it, Simms."

"Pushing it is exactly what I intend to do. Are you refusing my requests?"

"Maybe. Is that everything?"

There *was* one more thing. Jones had been very clear. Simms was to use his connections with Ballard to put the GMA off the scent. Tell them some unlikely story of what Forty Days were doing to divert them from the truth. That was presumably why Jones had contacted him in the first place, to exploit his contacts with Ballard. It would give Simms great pleasure to turn the tables on Forty Days. Not that Ballard had to know what was happening.

"One more thing," said Simms. "We meet up again. Later today or tomorrow. You pull me in for a chat. I spin you a yarn and don't tell you anything useful."

"Like normal."

"We insult each other and you threaten me. We argue and I make a complete fool out of you."

"And why would I agree to that?" asked Ballard, the threat clear in his voice.

"Forty Days must know you're monitoring me. They'll think it weird if you don't. The best way to cover up *this* meeting is to stage another when my plug-ins are back online."

"And you can have your fun with me."

"Just for show, of course. We put Forty Days off the scent and they think I really am working for them."

"Which you aren't, right? You're not trying to send me down a blind alley so you can work for Jones?"

"Do I seem like a religious nut?"

"You seem like someone who'd do anything to survive."

"Look, I'm taking a big chance for you here. I'm risking brain damage and my chance of staying on the list. What the hell do I have to do to convince you?"

Ballard stared at him for a moment. He sighed. "OK, so what's your brilliant plan?"

"How long does it take to morph your face into someone else's?"

"A month is best."

"What's the minimum?"

"Three days with a lot of pain."

"Three days it is, then. I'll give you video of the person you're to impersonate. I assume you can surgically extract their plug-ins, too? Embed them in your own brain?"

"Who are we talking about here, Simms?"

"Gideon Jones. He operated on my brain in this room. It's time I got my revenge on him, too. I'll get him here. You incapacitate him and grab his ID. Then you can get into their inner sanctum."

"Why three days? What's the hurry?"

"Jones said he had other hunters. If one of them gets the DNA first the whole thing is off. For you and for me. I think I can get the code I need in that time. When I'm done I'll contact Jones. He'll come here to collect and you strike."

"Forty Days has chapters the world over. They must have nukes everywhere, too."

"They aren't going to press the button if they don't have their twelve saints. Get to them and you put an end to Boneyard."

"A thousand things could go wrong with this plan, Simms."

"Yeah. And everyone's going to die if we do nothing. What choice is there?"

"One condition," said Ballard. "We tag you so we know exactly where you are at all times."

"Another bug. Just what I need."

"It's nothing personal. We just don't trust you, you see."

"It'll look suspicious to Forty Days."

"They'll have no idea. It will be completely isolated from theirs."

"I'm not going to let you operate on me."

"It doesn't have to be in your brain. Somewhere under your skin will work fine. I'll let you inject it. You seem to like injecting yourself."

"You haven't already got me tagged?"

"Trust me, we've had better things to do with our time."

So, maybe not the GMA shadowing him through the jump network. It didn't matter much now. Simms nodded in consent. "Want to know the amusing thing here, Ballard? You're going to have to help me break the law. Turn a blind eye while I track down this saint. After everything, that's pretty funny."

"Just make sure you play your part."

"I will. Now get lost. My vision is starting to return to

normal and I don't want to have to look at your face sober."

Ballard stood up. "Oh, one thing. When we have our pretend chat I may have to knock you about a bit. Inflict a few bruises. To make it look believable, you understand."

"Yeah, yeah. I understand. Now fuck off before you start scaring the neighbours."

XIX

Another day, another church. Still, that was dead saints for you. But the Cemetery Church of All Saints thirty kilometres south of Prague was *weird*. Simms stood in the arched gothic doorway of the place, trying to take it all in.

There were human bones everywhere. Chandeliers of femurs and delicate, curving ribs hung from the ceiling. Crucifixes carved from bone stood on the altar. The pillars holding up the vaulted ceiling were columns of skulls. And in case anyone failed to notice the decorative scheme, a carefully assembled pyramid of bones lay in each of the chapel's four corners.

It was an ossuary, filled with the bones of dead medieval pilgrims. A boneyard. Ironic, really. Quite why anyone would bother escaped him. The scene was like something from his nightmares: the ones he'd been having since learning what Forty Days actually intended. In his dreams, the whole Earth was like this. Drying skeletons blowing in the wind, horizon to horizon. An entire archaeological layer of bones.

Finding the sacred remains of Saint Gustav was not going to be easy. He'd imagined turning up and quietly stealing a few metacarpals while no one was looking. But there must be the bones of hundreds of thousands of people here. Which made it the perfect hiding place.

Simms approached the altar, hoping to see a casket or something equally precious. Nothing. And this was his last shot. The three days were nearly up. He'd blown most of it lurking around Rome and Istanbul and Madrid, looking for a way to get access to the remains of one of the names on the list Forty Days had given him. He'd got nowhere. Bombproof security again and again. Which was possibly his own fault. Since his adventures in Sienna, it seemed churches were being more careful, upgrading their security, doubling their guards.

Then he'd unearthed a scan of an old manuscript about Gustav, patron saint of some god-damned-thing or other, whose remains had been dispersed across Christendom in the fifteenth century. His bones sold off to various churches to satisfy the growing pilgrimage trade. Gustav was on the list. Most of the unfortunate man's remains had been lost, but his left hand had been brought here. Its touch was said to heal the blind and the mad. It had seemed worth a shot. The Cemetery Church of All Saints had little in the way of high-tech security. It was off the jump network, off the beaten track. So he'd come to Prague and hired a car, an actual car like the old days. An hour's drive through wooded, steep-sided valleys had brought him to the chapel.

"May I help you?"

A voice from behind him. Simms resisted the urge to whip round. He had to stay in role. He turned slowly. A priest watched him from halfway down the nave: an old, gaunt man, his hair white and his pale skin stretched over his bones as if a life spent among the skeletons was turning him into one.

"Forgive me, Father," said Simms. "I'm a pilgrim from Vienna. The door was open so I entered." Simms had considered reassuming the guise of Felippe Lombardi for the job, but had decided against it. It was quite possible the authorities wanted to speak to the mysterious Italian. Now, Simms was a Viennese businessman named Johannes Berg. He hadn't had the time to perfect his back story and accent, but it would hopefully suffice.

"Our door is always open," said the priest. "Are you

here to see the bones?"

The place was something of a tourist attraction, despite its remote location. Weird, but there it was. But Berg was no idle tourist. He was a devout pilgrim. A pilgrim badly in need of a miracle.

"No I… I've come in search of the holy remains of Saint Gustav. I read about them and their miraculous powers. I have brain cancer, Father, and I thought perhaps their touch might help."

The priest's expression softened visibly. They must get all sorts coming in here, tourists and crazies. Simms almost regretted fooling him like this.

"The church is rather lukewarm on medical miracles these days, my son," said the priest. He walked closer to Simms. Something looked to be wrong with one of his legs. He stepped forward with his left foot then dragged his right foot to join it. It didn't bode well for Gustav's healing qualities. The priest worked his way right up to Simms. "I'm afraid there can be no guarantees."

"Of course, of course. But I think I would feel better for… touching the relics. Praying over them." Was that what you did? Now that he thought about it he didn't actually know how this was supposed to work.

"That can be arranged, my son."

"The relics are here? Somewhere among all these other bones?"

"They are. If you know where to look." A twinkle in the old man's eye suggested he enjoyed his little game of hiding the sacred remains. He stood looking at Simms, waiting for something.

Of course. That was how it worked. Not a demand for payment, but an expectation. It was a trade like any other. Maybe if you didn't pay you didn't get to see the relics. Or you didn't get to see the real relics. And Forty Days would be watching all this carefully. He couldn't take any chances.

"While I'm here I would be delighted to make a

contribution towards the chapel's upkeep, Father."

"We are always in need of funds, my son. God's love is free and unconditional, but sadly our work among the needy is not. And it costs a fortune to keep these old buildings upright."

Simms pinged across a couple of K. He had no idea if the figure was ridiculously high or insultingly low. Judging by the smile that lit up on the old man's lined face, it was the former.

"If you'd like to walk with me, my son."

Simms followed the priest to a side door. "Do many pilgrims come to see the holy relics?" he asked. He'd spent the last three days terrified some other genehunter would beat him to the deal.

"Some. Not so many as there used to be," the priest replied. Simms longed to ask him who had come recently, what their names were, what they looked like. But he dared not. Hardly in character.

They passed through an ancient wooden doorway the colour of ash and out into the graveyard that surrounded the church. Simms found himself in a surreal forest in miniature: tall stone crosses and statues and gravestones, all elaborately carved. The priest weaved his way among them with his awkward halting step. Simms followed slowly and patiently, head down, like a good pilgrim.

They stopped outside a mausoleum: a squat, square building decorated with carved angels, their faces eroded away into blankness. A sturdy iron gateway protected the entrance. The priest pulled a rusting key from inside his robes and pushed it into the lock. It turned with a grating squeak. He heaved open the doors. Simms expected him to light a flaming torch but, instead, the man flicked a switch inside the building to reveal a flight of stone steps leading down into the ground. Simms could smell the age and decay breathing up at him.

Underground, Simms expected to see crumbling stone sarcophagi lining the walls, caked with cobwebs and the dust of ages. Instead there was a sea of bones, countless in number, filling the underground vault to waist height. No attempt had been made, here, to arrange and decorate. The bones must have been tipped in from above. How many pilgrims had there been, walking these roads to see the holy remains? He was only the latest of so many.

A narrow pathway had been left through the boneyard, ancient wooden baffles holding back the landslides of bones. The priest walked that way now. Simms followed. The damp air was cold on his face. Skulls watched him in open-eyed astonishment as he passed by. The priest stopped at a low altar in a cleared patch of floor at the far end of the mausoleum. A polished metal casket stood on it, quite small, decorated with red and blue stones.

"This is the reliquary," said the priest. "Our greatest treasure."

"Is it permitted for me to see the bones, Father? Perhaps the touch of them will help."

The priest considered, clearly uncomfortable about the idea. Simms, briefly, thought about knocking him out, grabbing the bones and leaving. He could do it. Perhaps he would have, once. But he didn't want to. The man looked frail and weak. He didn't deserve to be treated like that. And besides, he told himself, Forty Days was watching every move, and they wouldn't approve.

Simms was about to suggest another contribution to church funds when the priest relented. He touched Simms on the arm, his fingers bent like the probing beak of some bird. "I think that would be allowed, my son."

The reliquary wasn't locked. The priest opened it up to reveal the bones of the saint, almost a full set of carpals, metacarpals and phalanges, arranged in the approximate layout of a hand. They *looked* old, but that didn't prove anything. Simms shrugged to himself. Bones were bones. So long as Forty Days was convinced.

"Thank you, Father," he said. He knelt down, preparing to pray. That was what you did wasn't it? He hoped the priest would approve and leave him in peace. After a few moments he heard the old man's step-drag, step-drag as he made his way back above ground.

When the slow footsteps had ascended the stairs and disappeared, Simms burst into action. He turned, rose and began to search through the mountain of bones for replacements he could place in the reliquary. It didn't matter, did it? Any effect the bones had was in peoples' heads. As long as they thought they were holy bones, they were holy bones. While he was searching, he also collected ten or twenty small, random bones into a separate pile. Carefully, his back to the door, he tipped the contents of the reliquary into the plastic vial he'd brought for the purpose. Then he dropped the random assortment of little bones into the second, identical vial he'd brought. Finally he began to lay out the fake hand and finger bones he'd assembled into the correct arrangement within the reliquary. If you looked closely it was clear the bones didn't belong together. He just had to hope no one did.

The click of the blaster behind him stopped him dead. Blasters didn't need to make a sound. People did that when they wanted to let you know they were there and had a gun pointed at you. Simms got the message. He rose slowly and turned.

Devi stood in the middle of the mausoleum. So. No wonder she hadn't gone out of her way to help him. She wanted her own name on the Forty Days list.

"Devi," said Simms.

"Simms," said Devi.

"I guess this is where you threaten to blast my head off if I don't give you the bones of our friend Gustav," said Simms.

Devi shrugged apologetically. "Business is business. You know how it is."

"Uh huh."

"We both knew it would come to this sooner or later, didn't we Simms? You or me. Looks like it's going to be me."

"Looks like it," said Simms. "They offered to put your name on the list?"

"They did."

"Didn't have you down as a believer, Devi."

"I believe in *me*, Simms. What else is there?"

You learned a lot of things being a genehunter. How to reliably sequence DNA from a sample. How to cold-read a client and work out how much they could pay. How to hack a computer network and aim a blaster. Sleight of hand was a lesser known skill but there were times when it was invaluable. Simms worked some now, while continuing to talk.

"So," he said. "I toss the vial over to you and you escape with it?" He held the plastic vial up. But it was the *other* vial, the one he'd prepared in case something like this happened. "Just like that?"

"Just like that, Simms. And since it's you, instead of killing you I'll lock you down here. Assuming you escape you get to live until the bombs start falling."

"And if I refuse?"

She shrugged. "Then you get to live about ten more seconds. And I still leave with the bones. But filled with crushing remorse."

Simms paused, playing his role. He had to make it look like he was trying to think of a way out.

"Now, Simms," said Devi. "Before Father Death returns."

Simms scowled and tossed the vial to the side of her, onto one of the mountains of bones.

"Really, Simms," Devi said. "Is that the best you can do? I expected more."

Keeping the blaster trained on him, she began to clamber up the hillside of bones, wading knee-deep through shifting, rattling remains. Great drifts clattered down onto the cleared pathway. It looked like hard work.

Simms began to edge forwards, towards the door. He

moved slowly, arms held up to show he was no threat. He got about half way when Devi stopped him with a wave of the blaster. "No you don't. You're staying down here. You know I'll shoot if I have to."

"Oh, I believe you."

She was nearly at the top of the pile now, up to her knees in bones. She glanced down to reach for the vial, not watching him for an instant. Simms took his chance and ran for the stairs. It would take her only a moment to see what he'd pulled. To see the microbomb hidden among the random bones in the substituted vial.

"Simms!" she shouted.

He was nearly at the stairs. He glanced back. Devi stood trying to pull her legs free of the bones that held her.

"Sorry, Devi," he called. "Business is business. You know how it is."

She hurled the vial towards him. She had a good aim. Simms batted it away onto the pile of bones. He was about to turn and race up the stairs when the device exploded.

The mountain of bones where the bomb had landed came alive, erupting like an angry genii. The blast threw Simms backwards onto the steps, jarring his spine. A hailstorm of white shards, jagged as knives, drummed scattershot into him. Devi screamed. Then she stopped screaming. He'd covered his face with his hands but now he peered out to see what had happened. The pathway through the room was gone. The mausoleum was a sea of shattered bones. Devi stood there half-submerged, slumped forwards like a discarded toy. Blood stained the white bones around her. She didn't move.

"Devi?"

There was no answer.

"You or me," he said quietly. "Looks like it's going to be me. Sorry, Devi."

He turned and scrabbled up the stairs. Although they were underground the explosion would have been heard – or at least felt – all around the church. He had to get away before anyone decided he was responsible. Above ground, he saw the priest emerging from the chapel door. Fortunately the old man couldn't move quickly enough to stop him.

Simms turned and ran for the car he'd left parked in the roadway. Another – presumably Devi's – stood next to it. His vehicle activated as he approached, its doors opening to admit him. He instructed the machine to drive to Prague at maximum speed then sat back, breathing rapidly, hands shaking. He looked around as the car accelerated onto the main road in a plume of dust. He caught a glimpse of the white priest, waving an arm in the air, but there didn't appear to be any other pursuit. Still, he had to move as quickly as possible. Get far away. Escape into the anonymity of the jump network.

He held up the vial to examine. The real vial. Twenty-eight human bones, no different from the countless billions that had ever existed. He swallowed hard. They'd cost a lot to acquire. He placed them into his DNA sequencer. Samples this old would take time. He let the device work and sat staring out of the window, not really seeing the scenery that flashed by.

✕

He was striding through the Vaclav Havel Jump Station in central Prague when the sequencer finally reported success. 98% certainty. That was something. But by now he was desperate to jump away. He imagined police officers and other genehunters everywhere, suspected every passer-by who happened to catch his eye. But first he needed to get word to Forty Days. Get this whole thing over with.

He pinged Jones. "I have the DNA."

Jones replied immediately, like he'd been expecting the call. "Yes I know, Mr. Simms. We'd like delivery now, please."

"The stackroom."

"I shall be waiting. Don't delay."

There was a note of excitement in Jones' voice that sent a shiver through Simms. "I'll be there. Make sure you are too. I want you out of my head now."

Simms cut the connection and stepped with relief into the safety of the jump network, instructing the system to give him a single-hop to Euston.

✕

He stepped out at the other end and immediately knew he wasn't in London. Someone had diverted him. Again. Damn, he hated that. The GMA, keeping him out of the way while they ran their sting on Jones? But, no. He'd seen this place before. Not Ballard. An underground storeroom. Bare walls, harsh lighting, no windows. The sort of place people walked into and didn't came out of. The room he'd stood in while Raul Cahn extracted Stella Stiletto from her eternity in the jump network so Simms could sample her DNA.

MegaMeta. *They* were the ones shadowing him. That explained the privileged encryption keys. How had he missed that?

Raul Cahn stepped out of the shadows. A tall, fit looking man with silvery hair, walking with the easy assurance of someone who always got his way. Which, as the Director of Mega Meta Corporation, he no doubt did. He wore a smart suit, elegantly cut.

"Simms. Here we are again."

They were off-network. Forty Days wouldn't be able to hear anything. Which would make them real suspicious if he didn't get out of here now.

"Cahn, I don't have time for this. Trust me, you really don't want to stop me. I'm in the middle of saving the world."

Cahn looked amused as he sauntered closer. He wasn't coming too close, though. Probably another force-wall between them. "Saving the world, Simms? Really?"

"With the GMA. A group of fundamentalists called Forty Days are planning to nuke the planet." He held up the sequencer. "I know it sounds crazy, but this DNA is the key. With it we can gain entrance to their compound and stop them."

"And this is the best story you can come up with?"

"Speak to the GMA if you like. Speak to Agent Ballard."

"Yes, of course. I'll contact the authorities and say I've captured a genehunter called Simms in order to kill him. Do you really imagine I would do that?"

It was a fair point. Simms weighed up options. Cahn looked to be alone. No weaponry visible. But he'd have an array of blasters and killer-rays at his disposal. The obvious way out was back through the jump node Simms had arrived by. He sent software probes into it, looking for an exploit.

"Ah, now you're trying to hack the node," said Cahn. "Trust me, that isn't going to work. We *own* the jump network."

"OK," said Simms. "So what are you going to do? Shoot me or try and bore me to death?"

Cahn shook his head. "Oh, I'm not going to kill you, Simms. No, I've something much less messy in mind. You can join Ms. Stiletto. The node behind you *has* been reprogrammed. It is now an entrance with no exit."

"And the facts about Alex? What I said before still holds true. I disappear and the information about your affair and your unknown son gets released to the media."

"You don't pay attention to the business news, do you?"

It was true. He didn't. He had taken his eye of this particular ball. He shrugged. "I try to but then the boredom kicks in."

"Well. If you did manage to keep up, you would know the news about my situation is now in the public domain.

A straightforward piece of media manipulation. A few dire rumours leaked and then, when the time was right, a reveal of the truth that left everyone underwhelmed. So you see, you have no hold over me."

A cold dread trickled through Simms' veins. He was running out of options. He checked on the scans he'd sent into the jump network. He got nothing; the node was locked down tight. His only chance was to blast his way out. He had plenty of firepower and Cahn must have his own jump node somewhere. Question was, could he smash through those defences? It didn't look good, he had to admit.

Cahn, meanwhile, seemed to be enjoying himself immensely. He smiled his widest, corporate video smile. "You should be grateful to me, Simms. I'm giving you eternal life. Of sorts."

"Yeah, great."

"Ah, but now you're no doubt thinking you'll never see your daughter again. I'm not an evil man, Simms. I'll make you a promise. Every year, I'll get you materialised out of the network for a minute so you can see the latest video of her."

"Why would you do that?"

"So you can see her grow up. Grow up, grow old and die. Her whole life flashing by without you. Her whole life spent thinking you abandoned her, didn't even care enough about her to say good bye."

Simms pulled a blaster and set it to full power. Cahn hadn't come within ten metres. Most likely, the force-wall, if there was one, was that far away. He should be relatively safe from any counterblast. He aimed at Cahn's smiling face and let rip.

The bubble surrounding him roared into life at the impact. It flamed red, absorbing and distributing the blaster energy with a *whump* and a whining scream that rose in pitch until it was no longer audible. Simms fired again. And again. Each time the sphere flared brighter. Each time it held and Cahn stood there beyond it, calmly watching.

Simms stopped firing. This wasn't getting him anywhere.

"You know," said Cahn. "We are passionate believers in the freedom of the individual at MegaMeta. So I'm going to give you a choice. The sphere containing you and the jump node will now start to contract. You can choose to stay out of the portal and be crushed or you can choose to step inside. It's up to you."

The curving wall of the sphere was definitely nearer. Perhaps he could overload it. Punch through it. Aiming past the node in order to shield himself from some of the blast, he unleashed everything he had, spending his gun's fuel cell in one explosive burst of energy. The force-wall raged and seethed with the impact, but held. It rushed towards him, now, the heat of it painful on his face, its light blinding. Simms suddenly had only moments before it reached him.

"Cahn!"

No answer. Raul Cahn hadn't heard or had already left. Only one option. Simms threw himself forwards into the gateway. His last thought was something like resigned amusement. Damned jump networks. He'd never trusted them.

※

He fell out of the network at Euston, one of the gateways on the new twenty-four by twenty-four array. What the hell had happened? He checked the time. Thirty minutes had passed. He could still feel the heat of the raging force-field prickling his face. Yet here he was. Had Forty Days come to his rescue after all?

Then he saw. Across the thronged atrium, a man leaning casually against the wall, watching him. The man turned and left. Simms had been shadowed by enough law enforcement officers over the years to recognize one now.

The GMA. They'd been watching the node, waiting for Jones. They must have spotted he'd gone offline thanks to Ballard's bug and gone after him. Which meant the GMA had saved his life. God damn, he'd never hear the end of it. Simms pushed through the crowds to get out onto the street.

He half-walked, half-ran through the familiar London streets. No one apprehended him. No one even followed him. He reached the stacktower out of breath but unharmed. Better still, the lift was still working. He gave it his floor and leaned against the metal wall while it juddered into life. Twenty floors up it stopped. The doors crept open. Simms put his hand on another blaster in readiness, expecting attack. There was no one there. He was being paranoid; the lift had broken down again, that was all. Swearing to himself, he set off to climb the remaining twenty stories.

Jones was waiting in the stackroom. For once he wasn't sitting on the sofa, but gazing out of the window. His bland expression was the same as ever as he turned to face Simms. "So, Simms, you have the DNA?"

"You know I do."

Jones nodded. "Your delay in the jump network puzzles me. You were offline for thirty minutes. Where were you?"

"I wasn't anywhere. A glitch in the system. I wouldn't go near those things if I were you. They're evil."

"A mistrustful man might think you'd devised some clever means of consorting with the authorities without us knowing."

Simms kept his expression as neutral as he could. They couldn't suspect anything, could they? "I was held up in the jump network, Jones. You want logs to prove it?"

Jones began to pace around the room, picking up items and studying them, like he'd never seen a whisky bottle or a coffee cup or a blaster cell before. He stooped to examine the marker pen. He sniffed it then placed it carefully on the table. It occurred to Simms the room was even more trashed than usual. Had Jones been searching for something?

"Logs can be edited," said Jones.

"Look, do you want the code or not?"

Jones didn't answer for a moment. Perhaps he was praying for divine guidance. Perhaps he was having fun making Simms feel uncomfortable. The effect was the same either way. "Very well. Give me the sample."

"Terminate the bug in my head first. Then you get the DNA."

"You still don't trust me, Simms?"

"I trust you about as much as you trust me."

Jones sighed. "As little as that? Very well. I'll send the destruction codes now."

As before, a wave of nausea washed over Simms. Disembodied faces loomed up to him while creatures from the depths of the ocean bellowed and wailed in his ear. Then everything returned to normal. Or as normal as they ever got.

"Now the sample, Simms."

Simms shrugged and handed across the vial.

"Excellent," said Jones. "You have done well. I shall return to Forty Days with the sacred DNA of the twelfth saint. Truly the end days are upon us." He turned and strode towards the door.

"Wait," said Simms. "You haven't told me what to do to escape the destruction. Where do we go?"

Jones smiled his little regretful simile. "Ah, yes, I'm rather afraid there has been a change of plan there."

"What the fuck do you mean, Jones?"

"We've had serpents in the Garden of Eden before. I think, on reflection, we should leave you off the list."

"You bastard." Simms pulled his blaster yet again and aimed it at Jones. There was still no sign of Ballard and his ambush. He was on his own. "I thought you said you didn't lie?"

"Yes," said Jones. "But unfortunately that was a lie. Really, for someone so evil, you can be quite naïve."

"I'm going to kill you now, Jones. Or maybe I'll wound you and take my time over the killing part."

"Try if you must. You know it's not going to work."

Simms pulled the trigger, the blaster targeted right between Jones' eyes. Precisely nothing happened apart from a quiet *whirr* from the gun. He tried again. And again. Somehow, Jones had persuaded the supposedly secure electronics not to fire.

Jones, standing over by the door, started to laugh. A deep, roaring laugh. The sound stopped Simms. He'd never heard Jones laugh. *Smiling* seemed to take all the man's effort. On the other hand, there was something familiar about that laugh. He'd heard it before. Realisation dawned.

"Ballard. God-fucking-damn."

"Ah, Simms, Simms. I thought you were supposed to be smart."

"You think this is a good time to start playing games?"

"If it means seeing your face when you think you're going to die, then yes. Wouldn't miss it for the world," said Ballard.

"How long have you been here?"

"Couple of hours. Jones turned up early. Nasty fucker. Took eight of us to subdue him. We operated on him right here while you were lazing around in the jump network."

"He's here?"

"On your kitchen floor."

Simms strode into the kitchen. There was Jones, the real Jones, just as Ballard had said. He lay on the floor, head bathed in the blue light of an antiseptic field. A neatly stitched wound stretched from his ear over the top of his head. Two other GMA operatives stood over him, one checking vital signs on a monitor, one sipping coffee from Simms' espresso machine. Both agents bore signs of injury.

"How did you contain him?" asked Simms. "The guy

was unstoppable."

"Not to us," said Ballard. "You don't get it, do you? You think you're so clever with your illegal plug-ins and your military blasters. We're the GMA, Simms. We're an arm of the state. We have access to technology you haven't even dreamt off."

"You still needed me to catch him."

"You played your little part. Once we'd rescued you from the jump network."

"And will he survive?"

"Oh yes. We've made sure of that. Otherwise we couldn't lock him up for the rest of his life."

"And you're now his clone? Electronically I mean?"

"I am."

"You've recovered quickly from the operation."

Ballard snorted with amusement. "I've had his plug-ins imprinted onto the blanks I carry in my head. A simple electronic process."

"You can do that?"

"Of course we can do that. Only an idiot would let someone cut their head open with a knife to have a chip embedded. Oh, wait, that's what you did wasn't it? Twice."

"I didn't have any choice."

"You always have a choice, Simms. You tell yourself you don't to try and justify your decisions."

"And you think you have enough firepower to take on Forty Days?"

"Oh, we have the firepower, Simms. We're going to bring the wrath of God down on them, believe me."

Ballard turned to leave. The other GMA agents followed, carrying the unconscious Gideon Jones between them. Simms was about to warn them the lift had broken down, but thought better of it. They'd find out for themselves.

When he was alone he looked around his stackroom. It really was trashed. Jones must have put up quite a fight. When he had time, he really must replay the video of *that* little skirmish. It would make for a fun evening's viewing. But right now he had more important things to do. Events were moving quickly and he didn't want to be left behind.

His first act was to upload the video he'd recorded of Raul Cahn's little ambush to the public networks. Also the video of their earlier meeting, when the man had threatened to kill Eloise. Something like that would get round fast. Cahn's public image as a polite, God-fearing family man would be destroyed. As would his career.

Next, Simms pinged Arizona. To his surprise he got an immediate response.

"Nemesis? Are you involved in this assault?"

"Assault, Simms?"

"Come on, I know all about it. Forty Days. The GMA will obviously have informed clONE."

"And if they have?"

"I want to be involved."

"I'm not sure that's a good idea, Simms."

"I've proved myself, haven't I? I want to be there to make sure they don't fuck everything up."

There was a pause in the communication link across the ether. Simms was beginning to think she'd gone offline when she replied. "OK. You can come. If you promise you'll follow my orders to the letter."

"Sure. Orders. No problem."

"And you'll need assault armour. Can you get over here now?"

"I'm on my way."

✕✕✕

Simms sat on the ground examining his left hand. The good news was it looked intact. The bad news was it lay about ten metres away from the rest of his body, severed by a blaster shot during the chaos of the attack on the Forty Days bunker.

Actually, he couldn't even be sure it *was* his. Quite a

few body parts lay strewn around the floor. Another boneyard. The fight still raged, red lines of blaster fire flickering through the smoke. He couldn't work out who was firing at whom. His med plug-in had knocked him out while his assault armour sealed his wound and he'd only just come round. He felt no pain. He felt, if anything, elated. Distant from reality. Chemicals natural and artificial flooded his bloodstream. He had to force himself to concentrate. He'd seen more than one person stagger to their feet with a stupid smile on their face only to be reduced to molecules by a well aimed blaster shot.

The assault hadn't gone well. The authorities had brought some seriously heavy weaponry to bear, but Forty Days had responded in kind. Two high-tech armies clashing in a confined space. It was a miracle any of them had survived. Maybe only he had.

He sat against the dais on which the cloning vats stood. When they'd stormed the bunker, Simms had followed Nemesis on a spearhead thrust through enemy lines to secure the clones, lying oblivious in their sarcophagi. It had worked at first. They'd ringed the vats with a solid defensive line. Then Forty Days reinforcements had jumped in and it had all gone crazy. Three minutes of explosive impacts, voices screaming in his head, blinding flashes, blaster lines tearing the world to shreds. And then the hit on his arm and unconsciousness.

He still held his blaster in his right hand. Hauling himself up on the lip of the dais, its gilding stained red and charred black now, he tried to see if anyone else was still alive.

He made out a shape in the centre of the ring. Someone large, impossible to say who. Simms crawled forward, blaster held ready. The shape resolved itself into two figures circling each other, both holding knives. One was Nemesis. No mistaking her dancer's elegance despite the wounds and scorch marks about her body. The other was a man: tall and powerful. He held out a crucifix, a sharpened Forty Days dagger. Simms recognized him. The guardian of the sarcophagi. Somehow he'd survived the assault.

Simms pulled himself to his feet, blaster levelled at the circling figures in front of him. Hopefully no one from either side would risk a shot at him here among the bodies. Nemesis and the guardian noticed him at the same moment.

"Simms," said Nemesis. "Shoot him. This whole ring has a jump node built into it. We'll lose the clones for ever. We'll lose everything."

The Forty Days priest, or whatever the hell he was, regarded Simms with the calculating look Simms remembered from before. "You're the one Brother Jones consorted with."

"That's me."

"You recovered the code of the twelfth saint. He went to retrieve it. And you betrayed him."

Simms targeted the man's forehead. At this range he couldn't miss, despite the shaking of his remaining hand. The software would steady his aim. "Right again."

"So you have the code with you. In your head."

"Yeah. So what?"

"Don't you see?" said the priest. "Don't you see God's hand at work here? This was meant to be. The twelve assemble. The twelve new apostles. The dawn of the new world is upon us. Shoot this demon and we can finally begin."

"And the fact I betrayed Jones?"

"Doesn't matter. None of it matters. None of *us*. Only the twelve are important. The new age."

"But you're on the list, right?"

"As you will be if you side with us. You and your family. I give you my word. Join us in our new Eden."

"Don't listen to him, Simms," said Nemesis. "Shoot him now. That's an order."

Simms hesitated. Here was another of those moments.

A moment of decision. What side was he on? The answer was obvious. No one's side. His side. He walked the line. He *could* still change his mind, side with Forty Days. It would make life a lot simpler in many ways. In truth, he was tempted to fire on wide beam and kill them both. No one would ever know. But then *he* wouldn't know either. Wouldn't know what his decision was when it came down to it. Wouldn't know who he really was. Sometimes you had to choose which side of the line you were on.

"Simms!" the two shouted in unison.

He made his decision. Took aim and fired. The blaster shot crackled through the heavy air and hit his target bang between the eyes.

)0(

Supporting each other, Simms and Nemesis hobbled towards the makeshift triage point the medics had set up. Behind them, clONE members swarmed around the vats, checking vital signs. Off to one side, the few remaining Forty Dayers were being lined up against a wall by assault troopers.

As Simms sat and had his stump cleaned up and bandaged, Ballard broke off from barking out orders to walk over. The GMAn's face was streaked with blood and his left arm, too, was injured, slung across his chest in a white bandage. As he approached, he held out his other hand suddenly, like he was pulling a blaster or a blade. Simms flinched, expecting an attack. But then he saw. Ballard wanted to shake his hand. His remaining hand.

"I suppose I should thank you, Simms."

"I suppose you should. Next time, though, do your damn job yourself, OK?"

Ballard, still gripping Simms' hand, squeezed tight. Painfully tight. The GMAn was strong, metabolically boosted, his grip strong enough to break a few bones if he felt like it. He smiled, both Ballard and Jones visible in his features.

"Get out of here, Simms," he said. "I don't ever want to see your face again."

He let go. Simms forced himself to shrug with feigned indifference despite the sharp pain in his hand. His plug-ins reported no broken bones but bruising to the tendons. He switched the pain off. It didn't matter.

"Yeah," he said. "And I don't want to ever see *any* of your faces again, Ballard."

✖

Simms followed Nemesis through the node and into the familiar arrival room at Arizona. The two stood aside as, one by one, the eleven cloning vats were wheeled through. Everything was very quiet.

"What will happen to them?" asked Simms. His voice was hoarse from the smoke. That and all the screaming.

Nemesis watched the vats being taken away. "They're the real victims in all this. They'll be assessed and looked after."

"And the fact they're clones of saints?"

Nemesis shrugged. "We'll tell them, of course. When the time is right, explain their whole life-story to them. What they make of their genetic past is up to them. They're free to follow it or ignore it or rebel against it. That's the whole point."

Simms nodded. The last of the eleven was pushed out into the bright desert light.

"Come on," said Nemesis. "There are three women waiting for you."

"Three women?"

"Yeah. Lucky you."

They limped along the dusty path together, away from the jump node to the little white houses clustering around their green oasis. Another beautiful day: the sort of stunning heat that made everything feel pleasantly slow and distant. As it always was here. It felt good on his bruises and cuts, like it was healing them. They were a long way from the mist and rain of London.

"So am I allowed to know your real name yet?" Simms asked. "Seems like I should."

"Actually, you do. It's Nemesis. Most people think it's a code but I just had parents who loved Greek mythology."

"Must have been tough growing up."

"You should talk to my sister Nymph."

"Right."

"I thought you were going to shoot me," said Nemesis.

"Loss of blood. I was having trouble seeing straight."

"So who were you aiming for?"

"Him. Obviously."

"You weren't tempted? With that DNA sequence in your head you could have named your price. You could have lived like a king in their brave new world."

"I'd have been bored within a day. Not that I thought about it."

Simms could hear the chortling of water now. Squinting through the bright light he could see who was waiting for him. One was a baby, one was a very old woman and one was Kelly.

Kelly stood in the dappled shade of the trees, holding Eloise in her arms. She looked less gaunt than before. Maybe she was getting more sleep. Her black hair flowed down over her bare shoulders and she wore an elegant white gown, diaphanous in the sunlight. Simms wondered whether that was intended for him. He saw her eyes focus on the bandages where his hand should be. He must look a real mess. He felt like a real mess. Still, she appeared to be smiling. Either that or she, too, was squinting.

Eloise, resting her head on Kelly's shoulder, regarded him with open suspicion. Next to the two of them stood Mrs. Douglas, leaning on her wooden stick, a woollen cardigan draped around her bony shoulders.

"Mrs. Douglas," said Simms. "You're here."

"I am. Decided I was sick of the London rain chilling my bones, so I had a little word with my friends. And I wanted to meet Eloise, especially. She's a darling."

"Jane's been invaluable," said Kelly, smiling at the older woman beside her. "Eloise has really taken to her."

"Tell me," said Simms to Mrs. Douglas. "Did you bring everything from London? Including your teapot?"

Mrs. Douglas looked puzzled. "Of course. Why do you ask?"

"Just wondered. You… made a nice cup of tea, that's all."

"Even in this heat you can't beat a cup of tea. Come round and I'll make you one." Mrs. Douglas – Jane – smiled at Simms and Kelly, like she approved of what she saw. "Well, I'll leave you in peace. Let me know if you want me to keep an eye on Eloise for a while." With a sly twinkle in her eye she turned and shuffled off around the pool of water to one of the other little houses.

"So what do you think of my granddaughter?" asked Simms.

"She doesn't take any crap," said Kelly. "I like that."

Simms nodded. He got it. "And how is Eloise?"

"She's good," said Kelly. "But you look like death."

"Thanks. Been through a lot. People keep trying to kill me."

"Yeah, go figure. I'm glad they failed, though."

"You are?"

"I am."

"Because we stopped Forty Days or because I survived?"

"Both those things. I heard what you did. Getting our names onto their list."

"I put you at risk as well. If the attack had gone wrong neither of us would have survived."

"But it didn't go wrong and we all survived." She

stepped forwards, regarded him for a moment. "So," she said. "No more hunting?"

He thought about Grendel, about everything he'd been through. Everything he was. He nodded. "No more hunting. I know what it's like to be hunted. I know what it's like to be caught."

She reached up to kiss him. Her lips were soft and warm and tasted of sugar and sunlight.

"You did well, Simms, you know that? For once in your life, you actually did the right thing."

"So we're good? I can see you again?"

Kelly definitely smiled, then. It was her old smile: the carefree, mischievous smile he remembered. "You can see me in the morning when we have breakfast together," she said quietly.

He studied her for a moment, making sure he understood properly. He touched her face with his hand.

She led him through the dappled shade into the house. Eloise studied him over her shoulder as they walked. Simms smiled, pulled a face, pulled another. Slowly, bit by bit, his daughter began to grin back at him.

※

Three weeks later, Simms stood at the door of a Cairo hospital side room. The same one as last time. He debated with himself what he should do, standing there holding the door handle with his prosthetic hand. The building hummed with quiet activity all around him. Footsteps approached and receded as a doctor or a nurse strode purposefully by. Simms let go of the handle, deciding to not to go in after all. He'd go back to Arizona. That was where he belonged.

But then, changing his mind again, he pushed the door open.

The medical paraphernalia keeping Devi alive looked familiar. A swathe of tubes and cables running from the machinery beside her bed to the body under the covers. Except this time there were more tubes, more machines. Devi was awake, her face as grey as concrete, numerous partially-healed cuts marking her face like some one had written runes on her in some ancient language.

"Simms. Come here to finish me off?" Her voice was a croak.

"I thought I already had."

"And now you've saved the world, got the girl and can live happily ever after."

"Something like that."

"Yet here you are."

Simms walked around the room, not looking at her.

"What do you want, Simms?" she said.

He shrugged, feigned an interest in the readout of one of the machines.

"Ah, you've come to tidy up loose ends haven't you?" said Devi. "So what's it going to be? Kill me or arrest me?"

Simms pulled a chair from a corner of the room, scraping it across the hard floor. He sat close to Devi. To her head, at least. He wasn't sure how much of the rest of her there was.

"Maybe I'm simply here as Simms."

"Simms the ex-genehunter."

"Maybe."

Devi's eyes narrowed as she studied him for a moment. Then a smile broke out across her face. The beginnings of a laugh, too, although the pain it cost her soon cut her off. "You're fucking insane, Simms."

"I am?"

"You've got everything you ever wanted. You're free, you've got money, you've found out who you are. And here you are, risking it all. Walking the line. You can't keep away, can you?"

Simms shrugged. She was right. Damn her. He loved being a genehunter. Despite everything, despite who he was. Here was the thing: it was fun. And even the crowd at the Double Helix might forgive him once they learned he'd saved the world. More or less.

"So," he said. "Between you and me. What are we working on?"

THE END

JUMPJACKER

No sign of Simms in this short story, but Jumpjacker is another tale of jump nodes, brain plugins and high-tech crime.

Newer Delhi Central Station, 14:02 India Standard Time

Ronan Mistry half-stepped, half-fell from the jump gate at Newer Delhi Central. His stomach lurched like someone had spent the last-minute whirling him around blindfolded. A heavy pain thrummed through his head. He hated the damn jump networks. The headache was a new thing but the gates *always* made him nauseous. He was old enough to remember the days when aeroplanes still flew in the sky. It took hours to get anywhere – which always amused young people – but at least your body wasn't smashed to a stream of bits and reassembled each time you wanted to travel.

He'd promised himself before, but this was definitely the last time he used the networks. At the very least he'd pay for a private jump gate next time. It wasn't like he couldn't afford it. It was this affectation of being a *regular* person. His humble beginnings; try as you might you couldn't stop being the urchin from the back streets of Delhi. From now on he'd use some of ShivaTech's wealth and get around in a little more comfort.

"Morning again, Mr. Mistry."

A security guard in a saffron-coloured turban looked like he was about to step over to help. Ronan didn't recognize the man, despite the apparent familiarity. He waved and managed a smile to say he was fine, didn't need assistance. The guards were there to look out for jumpjackers hitting travellers as they emerged from the network, not to lend a hand to travelsick old men.

Ronan tried to walk off in a straight line and failed badly, tried to stop himself vomiting and just about managed it. He swallowed down bitter fluid that suddenly filled his mouth. Tens of thousands of people thronged the station, dashing to and from the gate array, barging aside anyone in their way. He bounced off more than one of them, mumbling an inaudible apology. He found a stone pillar, its cool solidity welcome. He waited for his head to stop swimming, standing there panting like an old dog.

He watched as a group of uniformed soldiers pushed through the crowd: not private jump network guards but proper IndPol military officers, bristling with tazers and lasers and who-knew what else. There must have been an incident. Perhaps some unfortunate traveller *had* been jumped as they stepped from their gate. Ronan watched to see what would happen, whom they would arrest. He hoped there wouldn't be serious trouble. He was in no state to run.

There was a moment of horror as the truth of what he was seeing hit him. The soldiers weren't running towards the gates. They were running towards *him*. His stomach lurched in panic.

It was only then he saw Sageeta, his wife, hurrying along behind the soldiers, her sari trailing behind her like gossamer wings. She looked angry. She was *never* angry. The soldiers ran up to him then stopped, parting to let her through.

"Ronan. What in all the hells is going on? What are you doing?" Sageeta stood in front of him, hands on hips. The soldiers surrounded them now, a ring of steel pushing the swarming crowds back. They didn't appear to be arresting him. They looked outwards, like they were protecting him. But from what? He didn't understand anything that was happening.

"Sageeta. It is good to see you. I'm feeling a little ill."

"Never mind that, you old fool. What have you done? What is this madness?"

He shook his head. "I don't know what you mean. I've just come from my meeting in Capetown about the new Europe contracts. I haven't *done* anything."

"Stop playing these games," said his wife. "You're going to explain everything right here and now."

"Explain what?"

A looked of worry flashed across his beloved wife's features. She spoke again, in a low voice, as if afraid people would overhear. "Explain why half an hour ago you transferred one billion rupees from ShivaTech to some no-good accounts I've never heard of. The company is ruined, Ronan. *We* are ruined."

"What?"

"One billion rupees! Our entire holdings gone in a moment."

"It's not possible. I ordered no such transfer."

"Don't be ridiculous. Did you think you wouldn't be seen? You made the transfer from a bank in London. IndPol have the images of you arriving at Euston Jump Node. And the images of you getting *here* an hour ago, when that oh-so lovely young woman stopped to help you. Is that what this is all about? Have you come to this?"

Ronan waited for some of his wife's words to make sense, but they utterly refused to. What she was talking about? What young woman?

"This is all madness," said Ronan. "I've just left Capetown."

His wife shook her head, as if pitying him. "Then tell me, Ronan, what the time was when you left Capetown."

"About one o'clock our time."

"And the time now?"

"Obviously, about one minute later." But as he spoke he also consulted the clock plugin in his brain, just to check. The response came back immediately. The time was now a little past *two* o'clock. Somehow, impossibly, an hour had passed by since he'd left Capetown.

It made no sense. Ronan tried to speak, but no words would come from his mouth.

Newer Delhi Central Station, one hour earlier…

Ronan Mistry half-stepped, half-fell from the jump gate at Newer Delhi Central. His stomach lurched like someone had spent the last-minute whirling him around blindfolded. A heavy pain thrummed through his head. He hated the damn jump networks. The headache was a new thing but the gates *always* made him nauseous.

A security guard, recognizing him, nodded his turbaned head.

"Morning, Mr. Mistry."

Ronan managed only a mumbled response. The pain in his head grew sharper, like something solid being hammered into his brain. The great hall of the station lurched around him, a blur of colours and blaring sounds. He leaned against a pillar, the stone cool on his hands.

"You don't look well, sir. Why don't you sit down?"

A young woman had stopped beside him, concern clear

on her face. There were still one or two good people in the world. He tried to explain he was OK, that he just needed a moment. He sank to the ground, his back against the pillar.

The woman put a gentle hand on his shoulder and knelt beside him so that her head was level with his. The bindi on her forehead was animated in the modern fashion: a swirling red spiral. She spoke quietly into his ear. "Listen to me, you fucker. You are *not* going to recover from this. You are going to feel worse and worse. Soon the pain in your head will become unbearable. And do you want to know what that pain is? It's the feeling of your mind being *eaten*, old man. Do you *fucking* understand me?"

Ronan stared up at her. The young woman continued to smile, the worried look clear on her beautiful face. Had he imagined her words?

Her grip tightened painfully. "Do you understand me?"

He didn't, not at all. He shook his head. "What is happening?"

The young woman glanced around, making sure no one was too near. "Tell me how many children you have, Ronan Mistry."

"What? What does that…?"

"Just tell me. How many?"

"Two."

"Boys or girls?"

"Girls. Grown women, now."

"Names?"

"They're called…" He stopped. For some reason he couldn't recall their names. Both had waved him goodbye just that morning as he left for Capetown.

"What are their names, old man?"

"I don't … I don't know."

"And what do they look like? How tall? What colour are their eyes?"

"I don't remember."

"What was their favourite flavour of kulfi when they

were young?"

He shook his head. He didn't know. The pain filling his brain was a fog. A fog through which he could see nothing.

The young woman nodded her head, as if he had done well, given her the right answers.

"Very good. Now let me explain what is happening to you. A small alteration to your neural matrix was introduced as you rematerialised at the jump node. An artificial algorithm hidden amongst your normal brain patterns. Right now, it is chomping its way though your memories. Soon you won't be able to remember you even have children. In a few hours you won't know your own name. A few hours after that your brain's autonomous functions will start forgetting how to function. Your heart will stop beating and your lungs will stop pumping."

"No," said Ronan. "That's not possible." He *knew* it wasn't possible. You couldn't just alter people as they rematerialised without introducing major flaws. The ensuing corruption was always fatal. The brain was too dynamic, too fluid. The technology was years away.

"Oh, it's possible, old man," said the woman. "And it's happening to you right now. No doubt you are experiencing an excruciating pain in your head? That is one side-effect."

Was that true? The networks were a well-known trigger for migraines. Perhaps she'd just struck lucky. "No. I don't believe it."

"Then let me ask you this. What does the name Arvan J. Stanton mean to you?"

"He's … just someone I knew once. Years ago, at university. Why?"

"Did he ever give you any advice? Any words of wisdom?"

"Actually, yes. I remember very well. He told me that whatever I did in life I had to believe the young woman with the red bindi when she stops to help me at Newer

Delhi…"

He trailed off. His memory of those words was very, very clear. But why? It was years ago. It made no sense. And why would his old friend have even uttered such nonsense?

"Yes, you understand," said the young woman. "Arvan J. Stanton did not exist. Another alteration we made to your mind. An implanted memory."

"I don't believe it. This is hypnosis. Autosuggestion. Nothing more."

"You don't really believe that."

"Even if you have done this," he said. "Even if such a thing is possible, why? Why would you want to destroy my memories?"

"Oh, not *destroy*, old man. We aren't mindless thugs. We are artists. Your memories are all still there. Just encrypted. Locked away in your brain with a key only we know. And when you've paid us the two billion rupees, we will give you the key and you can have your brain back."

"Two *billion* rupees?"

"That's the price. ShivaTech can afford it. A man of your wealth really shouldn't use the public networks, you know."

The fog was lifting a little in his head now. He saw the obvious flaw in her proposal. And making deals, striking bargains was what he was good at. "So, when I pay you this fortune, you'll just drop round and fix up my brain for me? Set everything straight?"

"You'll need to make another jump. We'll spot you in the network and put everything right. There'll be no need to meet again."

"Yes, but why would you?" said Ronan. "Once you've got your money you'd be better off leaving me to die. Then all the evidence goes away. It's a perfect crime."

The young woman smiled. "You'll just have to trust us, won't you? You're hardly in a position to bargain."

He could see the faintest hint of worry in her eyes. You

learned to read people. "Actually," said Ronan, "I think I am. They're certain to *post mortem* me. I'm willing to bet your hacks to my brain – if they exist – will show up. That will raise suspicions. People might follow a trail that leads back to you. And I don't think you want to take that risk."

The brief frown of annoyance that flashed across her features told him he'd hit the mark. She nodded her head from side to side, trying to suggest indifference. "We'll take that chance for two billion rupees, old man."

He considered. He still didn't believe her. But if there was a chance she was telling the truth…

"I'll make you an offer," he said. "*One* billion rupees and I don't send the money until I'm fully restored to health."

"That's not going to work, old man."

"Ah, of course, because you were also planning to wipe all my memories of this conversation, weren't you?"

"Obviously. You'll be in no state to sanction further payments. You won't know anything about them."

"Then I'll give you half the money now and place half in an account in your name but which you can't access for twenty-four hours. That will give you time to restore me."

The woman studied him for a moment, looking for the flaws in the plan. He just had to hope she didn't know everything ShivaTech's systems *could* do. Finally, she nodded. She'd might not get all the money, but she'd decided even half a billion would be enough. As Ronan had calculated she would.

"Very well," she said. "But not in my name. Use Arvan J. Stanton, understand?"

"As you like. I'll have to jump to London to arrange everything."

"You remember your non-existent friend's old contact number?"

"For some reason, yes, I do. Very clearly."

"That's the account number for the first half of the payment. Make sure the new account is in his name, too, and we'll see it. And remember: in three hours time you won't recognize your own face in a mirror. So, don't fuck up."

She smiled and stood up. She lifted her scarf over her head to cover her features. "Oh, and be careful in the jump network, Ronan Mistry. There are some bad people out there."

She turned and strode away. He soon lost her in the teeming crowds.

Doctor Kay Alvarez was engrossed in an analysis of the fractal equations from her latest tests when her boss staggered in. She hadn't seen Ronan for nearly a year; these days the owner of ShivaTech didn't travel so much. Her delight at the sight of her old friend was immediately tempered when she saw the state of him. He was clearly struggling to stay upright.

"Ronan? What has happened? You look terrible. Shall I get a doctor?"

"You *are* a doctor, Kay. That's why I've come to see you." For a moment she caught a flash of her old friend's humour. Then he sank into a chair and held his head in his hands.

"We need to get you to a hospital," said Kay. "You know very well I'm not the right sort of doctor."

"Actually," said Ronan, "you are exactly the right sort. I need you to scan my brain and look for … anomalies."

"What do you mean *anomalies*?"

He appeared to be having trouble getting the words out. He was clearly in great pain. "Please," he said. "There isn't much time. I need you to do this *now*. There's this thing in my head. A … bad thing."

With anyone else she would have insisted on the hospital. But, as she'd come to learn over the years, Ronan generally knew best. "OK. Come with me."

Ten minutes later she had the live feed of his brain imaging in front of her. She sifted her way through the 3D map, looking for these mysterious anomalies. What was he expecting her to find? A tumour? A clot? A bleed?

"Anything?" he asked.

"Nothing. No damage at all. Wait. What the hell? *That* doesn't look right."

"What do you see?"

"These neuron patterns here in the hindbrain look almost … random." She turned to Ronan. "Is this what you mean? This corruption?"

"Is it spreading?"

She turned back and zoomed in. It took only a few moments to see it. She watched as more and more of the connections between the neurons realigned themselves. They switched from normal, organic arrangements into broken, disjointed fragments.

"It is," she said. "Advancing rapidly. Do you want to tell me what the hell is going on here, Ronan? Frankly, it's incredible you're even walking and talking."

Ronan nodded but didn't reply.

"Ronan? What has happened? What is this?"

With great effort, as if having to drag up ancient memories, he began to tell her the day's events.

When he'd finished she was silent for a moment. If she hadn't seen his scan she wouldn't have believed it. "Ronan," she said finally, "I'm so sorry."

He shook his head. "No. You don't understand. This is an incredible opportunity."

"What?"

"Whoever these people are, however they've done this, we need this technology. They're years ahead of us."

"It must be experimental," said Kay. "For all we know it only works one in a hundred times. One in a thousand. You're incredibly lucky just to be here."

"Yes, but think what we could do if we had this capability. If we could reliably edit people's images. We could cure diseases, do *anything*. We have to pursue this."

"Always the idealist, Ronan. You can't go ahead with

this; you're going to get yourself killed. Somehow, we have to stop the encryption of your neural matrix. Restore you somehow."

He shook his head. "The thing is, I've already instructed the bank to transfer the money."

"What?" she said again. She was beginning to doubt his sanity now. Was this the corruption in his brain speaking? "Ronan, this is madness."

"No, Kay. Listen to me. Listen while I can still think straight. OK, perhaps they'll talk their half billion and run. And then I am in serious trouble. But there's a chance they'll do what they said: intervene again to fix me so they can get the rest of their money, yes?"

"There's a chance," she said. "There's also a chance they'll zap your brain completely to cover their tracks."

"No. It will look too obvious. They're clever. Who knows how often they've done this? We need to stop them. You need to stop them."

"Me?"

"You'll know where I am in the jump network. You can track me among all the billions of images?"

She shrugged. "Sure, that we can do."

"And when they intervene – if they do – you'll be able to see it, yes? They must be using a hacked jump node. You'll be able to get a physical address. We'll be able to get to them."

She studied him for a moment. He was serious. He really meant to do this. "Ronan," she said, "this is a whole series of *ifs* and slim chances. It's not going to actually work."

He smiled through the pain. He actually smiled. "Maybe. *Or* we'll put a stop to a bunch of evil hackers and acquire technology ShivaTech could work wonders with."

"If by some miracle it works and they do wipe out your memories of all this, you're going to be pretty confused when you emerge from the jump network. You won't have a clue what's going on."

"I'll manage."

She shook her head. "I don't like it. I don't like it one bit."

"Then it's a good job I'm the boss. Consider all of that an order."

"Ronan, you haven't given me an actual order in thirty years."

"Then I'm asking. Please, Kay. If it goes wrong it hardly matters at this stage, does it?"

She studied him for a moment more, then relented with a sigh.

"Oh, and Kay?"

"Yes?"

"Please hurry. My head feels like it's going to damn well *explode*."

Ronan now lay on the hard floor of the station concourse. He couldn't make sense of anything. The same fragments of thought kept circling around in his brain. Somehow, he had lost an hour of his life. And one billion rupees. And now, it seemed, he was losing his mind too. He was finding it harder and harder to recall names, details, places. The pain in his head was a vast weight, crushing his memories beneath it.

Figures milled around him, their faces occasionally looming over him to ask him questions he couldn't hear. His wife was there, the anxiety clear on her face. For some reason he couldn't recall her name. That was bad. Paramedics buzzed around, shining lights in his eyes, giving him oxygen, checking his blood pressure. There were also soldiers. Lots of soldiers. Some stood in a ring around him, their black boots filling his vision when he opened his eyes. A group of them had just charged off for the jump gates on some suddenly-urgent mission. He didn't know why.

None of it made sense. Ronan groaned and closed his eyes.

"Can you see them? Have you got the trace?"

The IndPol officer stood over Kay. It was hard to concentrate with him standing there. These things required focus, concentration, not some armed grunt breathing down her neck.

Her hands moved through the display, sifting through the almost limitless threads, each representing a single person's journey through the jump network. She would only get one shot at this. They had to be careful. If the hackers saw they were being traced they would be gone and that would be the end of Ronan.

"There. That's them. This gate here."

"You're sure?"

"Of course I'm sure. That's why I said it."

"OK," said the soldier. "We're jumping there now."

"And I'm coming with you," said Kay.

"Sorry. No. This is a dangerous military operation. We can't be worrying about civilians."

"And I'm sorry, but I am coming," said Kay. "It's vital we recover the technology these people have. You do your job and we'll do ours, understood?"

The IndPol officer looked like he was about to argue, then backed down. Turning away, he began to bellow out orders to his troops.

Someone was touching his cheek, trying to rouse him. Ronan flicked open his eyes. He expected to see Sageeta but another woman's face was there. A woman he recognized.

"Kay? What are you doing here? You're supposed to be at work in London. I'm not paying you to just gallivant around the world."

"Long story. I'll explain later. Right now, I'm going to scan your brain for anomalies."

"You're going to do what?"

"Just be quiet. This is the first time I've done this in a

public jump station. Turn your head to the side then don't move."

Ronan did as he was told. He'd found that was best with Kay. Through a forest of soldiers' boots, he could see the jump node he'd emerged from *en route* from Capetown. More of the soldiers were surrounding it. He watched as a squad of them emerged, escorting some prisoners. Two women and a man. One of the women – young, a bright red bindi on her forehead – turned to look directly at him. She scowled. Ronan couldn't understand why. He'd never seen her before in his life.

He could hear Kay and Sageeta murmuring to each other, something about the readings on the brain scanner.

"Well," he said. "Would you two like to tell me what is happening?"

"There's good news and bad news," said Kay.

"What's the bad?"

"You're the same stubborn old man you were this morning," said his wife.

"OK. And the good?"

"Your brain is clear of anomalies," said Kay. "The decryption as you jumped worked. You're in the clear."

"I have no idea what you're talking about."

Kay ignored him. "With IndPol's help we should be able to recover the technology they were using. You were right. It looks pretty incredible."

"Technology?" said Ronan. "What technology? You're not making any sense."

Ronan levered himself up onto his elbows. The room wasn't spinning now. He thought he could probably stand. The pain in his head had subsided to a dull throb. Sageeta offered him an arm to help him up.

He looked back over at the gates. Damned jump network. They always made him sick. This was *definitely* the last time he used them.

22ND CENTURY GENIE

This was the original Simms story, published by the UK SF magazine Jupiter. Simms is recognizable in it, although many of the details of his world differ significantly. The jump network is here, as are Simms' brain-enhancement plugins, but there's no mention of the GMA or Forty Days or cIONE or MegaMeta. The good news for Simms is that both Devi and Kelly are here (although Kelly is called Jen and Eloise, Purity).

The story and themes in 22nd Century Genie are similar to those in The Genehunter, although there is a different tone to this earlier story. As you'll see, it's once again concerned with the recovery of the DNA of rock musicians, but in this story they are very well-known, real people. So well known that even Simms knows who they were...

Perhaps the biggest difference here is the ending. Without giving anything away, it's clear 22nd Century Genie was conceived as a single story. The ending makes that pretty clear. The events of this short story and of The Genehunter clearly occupy different, although closely-related universes. But that's fine. We're allowed to do that in SF...

I started with John. Lord John, Saint John, the apostle of Elvis in heaven. The others, Paul, George and Ringo, could wait. With John at least I knew I could get somewhere.

It was the church I turned to. People do in their hour of need. Most went for salvation, the reassurance of some meaning to it all. My needs were easier. All I needed was a 100% reliable image of the DNA of John Winston Lennon. Born Liverpool, Earth, 1940. Died New York, Earth, 1980, almost exactly one hundred and fifty years ago.

Gold letters above the arched doorway of the Holy Church of the Fabulous Four in Liverpool declaimed *All You Need Is Love*. The square outside was thick with tourists but inside it was cool and subdued. I gazed upwards, awed by the simple trick of soaring architecture. Everything was white marble. My footsteps echoed in the vast space as I walked towards the central stage. Worshippers, mostly alone, sat with their heads bowed. Music filled the church, something about *All across the universe*. I didn't know it. I should have paid more attention at school.

The man I had jumped up from London to see was taking the service. Candles, actual candles, were set all around the stage, flames hissing. He intoned solemn words from a book. From what I could see of his face through his long hair he looked bored. It was three years since I had tested a lesser relic for him. A vial of the blood of David Bowie, genuine enough. He had also shown me, eyes wide, their genuine Lennon remains. Hidden from the eyes of unbelievers were the blood-stained glasses he had been wearing when Mark Chapman gunned him down. Provenance beyond question. I'd made a mental note in case the information ever proved useful. Which it now was.

The ritual over, I followed the priest at a respectful

distance across the echoing floor to a side chamber. *Clergy Only*, it said on the wooden door. I pushed it open. I expected to see more bare stone inside, but it was a warm, well-furnished room. Father Daniel Jones sat on a soft chair, sipping a drink, clearly expecting me. He had put on weight. I bobbed my head towards him. Illuminated images of the Four peered down at us from the walls.

"Mr. Simms. Have you come to repent?" he asked, indicating a chair.

I smiled at him. He knew my views.

"A more earthly matter."

"Ah well. The church caters for all needs."

"In return for your help I'd like to make a donation. To church funds."

He looked sad but there was a smile in his voice.

"Our lord imagined that, one day, there would be no money. Alas, for now, there is still great need of it."

Thirty minutes later I was sampling DNA from the blood-stains on the glasses. It came out at a healthy 99.9% match against the known phenotype. I transferred a million credits to Jones's own account. The details at his end were none of my business.

As I left he shook my hand, his skin soft and slightly moist.

"Remember," he said. "The church is always here for you."

✕✕

Back in London I walked, actually walked, from Euston Jump Node to my stackroom in the badlands of Camden Town. I was feeling good. The job of a lifetime and I'd completed a quarter of it on the first day. I was set up for life. No more being pushed around. I could do anything: buy some land, buy some people, live like a *king*.

The streets were full of hurrying people. The city smelled, as ever, of shit and burning plastic. At least the sun was shining. I accessed the overlay plugin in my brain, picking out something expensive. I could afford it now. Soon, an augmented city replaced the decaying original. Trees lined spotless streets. The air smelled of roses. Contented people strolled smiling by. They were dangerous, these false realities. People got lost in them. But right now it was fine.

When I got back home my room was in chaos. Which was just how I'd left it. In some places the crap was three layers deep: half-finished meals furred with fungus balanced upon piles of clothes smothering papers and books. The bird, its feathers iridescent, lurched into clumsy flight as I entered. I'd stood on it a year ago and broken its wing. Now it spent its time absorbing energy before, obeying its programming, attempting to fly. Invariably it crashed disastrously and often quite comically. I liked it that way. This time it lurched in a tightening spiral and clattered into a picture of Jen and I, taken that day up the Eiffel Tower 2, her smiling face against the blue sky. The picture I'd been meaning to put away for months.

I sipped thick, bitter, real coffee. It had been a hell of a few days. I sat on my bed, the only free surface, and instructed my lifetime plugin to replay the previous day's concert. I wanted to be sure I hadn't missed anything.

✖

We floated ten metres above the ground, thirty metres from centre-stage of New Shea stadium. No doubt obscuring the view from the cheap seats in the stands behind us. Down below a sea of bobbing, disembodied heads filled the stadium.

James Cross himself greeted me. He was dressed in retro jeans and tee-shirt. He was a hundred years older than I was but looked about the same age. His features were elegant, his hair silver. My psych plugin couldn't read anything off his aura: no colours, no patterns, nothing except a fuzz of white noise.

"Mr. Simms," he said. "Good of you to come."

Maya was there too, gazing down on the people below us with sniper's eyes. She didn't acknowledge me.

We chatted about irrelevancies for a time. The concert started. It was my first. I don't get round to high culture much. On the stage the synthetic Beatles were met with a huge, swelling roar. John muttered a few words of thanks and they launched into the first song, actions synchronised perfectly to the music. Although every performance was different, I knew. Always random variations.

"George's guitar sounds louder," I said. Actually I couldn't tell. But brief research carried out *en route* had uncovered a few facts. A techie friend of a friend. It always paid to sound like you knew what you were talking about.

James Cross smiled and nodded his head. It was the opening for the real conversation.

"I'm told you are the best in your field, Mr Simms?"

"I try," I said.

"Well, we would like you to retrieve some DNA for us."

I did my legal duty and gave him the speech about the uses to which genetic material could be put. Maybe it was enough for him to show his friends a bunch of molecules and tell them who each one represented. But I doubted it. Not someone in this league. He was no mere collector; he had the sort of plans neither of us could admit to.

"We both know the law is irrelevant," he said. "But we can pretend if it makes you feel better."

"Who do you want?" I asked.

He looked back at the stage. They were playing *Twist and Shout* now, John's singing raw.

"Them," he said. "I want you to find me the DNA of The Beatles."

We talked details. Money no object for a guaranteed genome. He could afford it I knew. More research had confirmed that easily enough. He and Maya owned the rights to all Beatles music. And that was more money than you could begin to count.

As I was leaving, the concert over, Maya looked up at me, a distracted smile on her face as if she was half asleep. She spoke for the first time.

"Beware of the dog now, Mr. Simms."

Possibly she was mad. I smiled back but did not reply.

XIX

When the replay had finished I sat for a while in thought. The thought that I had missed something nagged at me. The first rumblings of a headache throbbed in my mind, making it hard to think. Eventually I gave in and slept.

I spent the next few days making plans, pursuing leads. Paul's DNA had to be extant as he had donated his body to science. George I had no idea about. Hair follicle maybe? Fans might have collected some. Ringo too: the last of the four to die but the one I had least idea about.

I trawled the net for hours on end. Being a Genehunter – a Genie if you prefer - is not the glamorous job you see in the synths. Mostly it's drudge work and talking to people who don't want to speak to you. Eventually I earmarked over fifty samples of *guaranteed genuine* blood. Also sweat and tears. And probably all worthless. The problem, of course, was getting anything reliable. Any fool could cobble a DNA sequence together and claim it was Jesus. Some of the low-grade stuff out there was just random numbers. I put out feelers, anonymous, making it clear I was only interested in verifiable code.

Finally, getting nowhere, I pinged Devi, the closest person I had to a partner. We had tried to kill each other at least three times. I tracked him down to a hospital in Cairo where they were cultivating him a new set of internal organs. His last job had gone badly wrong.

It was already evening by now. A hazy, misshapen sun was melting into the haze of the city skyline. My eyes ached though I'd barely used them. Cairo could wait. Instead, acting before I could stop myself, I tried contacting Jen. We hadn't spoken for a year. It took a while for her to answer.

"How did you find me?" Her voice quavered with emotion. Anger, most likely.

"It's easy if you know how," I said. "I need your help."

"Ah, of course. Business. I'm *fine*, thanks for asking."

"I'm sorry, Jen."

"What do you want from me now?"

"I wondered if some DNA might have washed up at the Refuge."

Given her views on what I did for a living, her response was predictable.

"You're fucking unbelievable," she said and cut the connection.

✕

By the following morning, two separate people were offering me Ringo, provenance beyond question, each requesting astronomical amounts of money. Which might be a good sign. I stood looking out of my window as I considered. London was grey, the stacktowers around mine washed away in a deluge of rain. Cairo was suddenly very appealing. I requested a copy of each sellers' proof and overlaid my way back to Euston for the jump. Distance was no object; the Crosses had provided an open credit for a jump network. A classy one too; there was even a chance I might get around without being reorganized into organic goo or held in buffer-limbo for the rest of my life.

I found Devi lying in bed in a white, airy room. It smelled of chemicals. A thousand tubes and wires snaked out from under his covers to a silver box on which an array of lights blinked rhythmically. He looked tired, deflated, his face more grey than olive. His brown eyes were blurry and indistinct but he grinned his familiar pained grin when I came into his room.

"How did you get in here?" he croaked.

"Told them I was a friend."

"You were always a convincing liar."

"Who were you hunting?"

He closed his eyes for a moment as if trying to remember.

"Blair. Those people are ruthless."

I didn't hang around. I knew he could zonk out any time. I gave him my story. As I talked, a cool breeze blowing through an open window brought with it the roar and rush of the city outside.

"So they signed you up too, did they?" he said.

"I'm competing?"

"The Crosses are no fools. Obviously going to correlate. You're the third I know of."

So much for being the best in my field.

"Who else?"

"Weston and Patel. Thing is, Weston's gone off the net completely now. Not sure about Patel either. You need to be careful, my friend."

"A man with no internal organs is telling me this?"

"I'm serious. George and Maya Cross don't fuck around. They're not nice people. Whatever they're up to."

"But can you help me?"

He smiled again, something like his old self twinkling away for a moment.

"I may have heard something."

Which was the cue to talk about money. I didn't haggle. We both knew the going rates. We agreed terms: half up front, balance on delivery. My com plugin registered an encrypted message. Jorge Ramon, 910th floor of the Diego Maradona Starscraper, Upper Buenos Aires.

"I marked this guy a year back. Your basic molecule collector, genuine but harmless. Has this private gallery, a portrait of each individual next to their crystal-encased

DNA. Madonna, Harry Clinton, Pope Joan, Gandhi and George, all cast-iron. Give him my name. I'm sure he'd be interested in trading for John."

Sometimes, all it took was knowing which people to ask and having enough money to pay them. It seemed too easy.

"Thanks," I said. "You're all heart."

He smiled again, weakly, and closed his eyes.

"Now fuck off and leave me alone," he said.

✕

A day later I stood gazing at a sparkling sea. The heat on my face was like someone punching me but a breeze blowing in off the Indian ocean made it bearable. I stood on a balcony on Isla Negra, the Cross's private island. *Yellow Submarine*, their sunrigger, lay at berth not far away, its prow rising and falling slowly as if it was asleep in the heat. A servant shuffled up to me with a drink of lassi on a silver tray, ice-cubes tinkling.

This was it, I thought. This was how I'd live once the job was over.

I filled the time with an idle fantasy. A place like this, lots of room, guaranteed privacy: it would be ideal for Jen's Refuge. I imagined us back together, the past forgotten, me idling away my days on the beach, she dividing her time between me and saving the world's GM victims. All those brain-damaged Elvises and broken Mandela-copies living out their remaining years in paradise. She would, of course, be full of gratitude. It would be beautiful.

I watched as a child, a boy, played on a patio some way below me. He batted a ball to and fro with a stick, occasionally whooping with delight as he succeeded in something only he could understand. I smiled at the sight of him.

"Mr. Simms."

It was Maya, standing next to me. She was dressed all in white. She looked as fantastic as James did, statuesque, the two of them a testament to expensive metabolic engineering. But up close there was an absence in her eyes. Her immaculate features were expressionless. I wondered what it took to get her excited.

"Your son?" I asked.

"Him? No. We bought him fifteen years ago and kept him biochemically stunted ever since. They're so cute at that age aren't they?"

"You insisted I report back every seven days," I said.

"Do you have anything for us?"

"Half the genome. John and George, guaranteed pure." I had toyed with the idea of stringing things out but they were probably watching me.

"Very good," she said. I sent the images over to her. There was a pause while she analysed them then she, in turn, paid me my 50%. In that instant I became a very rich man.

"I'll be back in seven days," I said.

She turned away from me while two guards lumbered up to escort me back to the jump node.

※

Back home, I put on some Beatles music as I worked: the more obscure stuff that academics pored over. I had to admit, it was growing on me.

I went back to basics. Ringo next. All I had to go on were the two offers of blood. I now had the documentation for both and they looked genuine. Still I was reluctant. You couldn't trust anyone.

The beginnings of another headache was soon thrumming through the veins in my brain. I sipped more coffee while my net plugin ruffled through data, terabytes of it streaming through my head. I worked through Ringo's medical history and over two hundred biographies and papers, looking for anecdotes or episodes that might give me an opening. I worked for six hours straight, sitting stationary with my eyes shut, but found nothing.

I was interrupted by someone contacting me. My com plugin registered the ping with a highly unexpected image. I was disorientated. It took a few moments to grasp what was happening.

"Jen," I said.

"I wasn't sure if you'd be around."

Her voice sounded hoarse and hollow, as if she had been up all night arguing. I wondered who with.

"Is anything up?" I asked.

"I wanted to speak to you again," she said. "You caught me off-guard the other day."

"I shouldn't have contacted you."

"No, you should. I've been meaning to speak to you. There's someone I'd like you to meet. Could you come over to the Refuge?"

Which made no sense. It was certainly possible they did have some Beatle clone there but it seemed incredible she would tell me.

"What's this about?"

"Can you just come over? Please?"

"Sure."

"I'll be waiting."

I sat for several minutes trying to make sense of it, but couldn't.

XIX

The Refuge was in the hills of mid-Wales. Once it had been a farmhouse sitting alone in a great bowl of a valley. Now it was pretty much a complete town. It was a surreal place, its streets filled with familiar faces. A Marilyn Monroe ambling by or a Saddam Hussein in full flow, declaiming to a non-existent crowd. All of them broken or damaged: some suffering from genetic disorders as a result of botched - and obviously highly illegal - conceptions. Most perfectly sound physically but mentally scarred by their experiences in private zoos.

Jen was standing at the edge of the jump node floor as I winked into existence. She was the same willowy, black-haired beauty but she looked taut, her features drawn into lines. My body remembered the clasp of her surprisingly strong embrace. Now, we merely greeted each other politely.

"This way," she said.

We walked down a street past lines of small chalets, each with a little square of garden at the front. The air was thick with the scent of grass. Like most people, I lived my life in cities, jumping between them when I had to, never setting foot outside. It was always a surprise to be reminded there were still places like this in the world. We stopped at a chalet with blue and purple walls, its door shut, its lawn overgrown. Jen lead me up the path to peer in through a small window.

Inside, a man with long, ragged hair sat at a piano. His back was to us but I could tell immediately who it was. He was attempting to play but clearly could not. Over and over his fingers found random discords. He stopped and started repeatedly, constantly surprised at hitting the wrong notes.

"He does that all day," said Jen. "For ten years now."

She held out a datafleck for me.

"Here is the DNA image of James Paul McCartney along with all the proof you'll need."

I was stunned. I looked into her eyes, trying to understand if this was some sort of test.

"I don't understand. Why are you giving me this?"

A look of pain writhed across her features, marring her beauty.

"Just promise me there'll be no clones."

What could I say? I nodded agreement.

"But why?"

"When I said there was someone I wanted you to meet, it wasn't him."

"Then who?"

"She's this way."

She strode back out of Paul McCartney's garden. I followed, elated and confused at the same time. The road opened out into a square, one side taken up by the original farmhouse. Next to it was a taller white building with many windows. We walked up a set of stone steps.

"This way."

We clacked down a long corridor. A doctor strode by, head down, not making eye-contact. We stopped at a door which lead into an anteroom. Next to the inner door was a window looking into a patient's room. The bed marooned in the middle of the room was tiny: just a cot. A baby lay there, its body just a lump huddled underneath the blankets. It lay unmoving but with its eyes wide open.

"Who is this?" I asked. Even as I spoke I felt my insides clenching up. I suddenly knew who it was.

Jen sighed.

"It's our daughter."

"I don't..."

"I should have told you, I know. But her hold on life has always been so... tenuous. She had to be resuscitated at birth. And four times since."

"She's sick?"

"Merimans. She won't survive the next crash."

I was numb. I accessed my plugins without thinking.

"It's curable with *in utero* gene therapy," I said.

Jen said nothing. She had rested her forehead on the glass of the window and was crying silent tears. All she could do was shake her head.

"She wasn't treated?"

"I was so sure of myself," she said. "So Mother Earth fucking *natural*. Don't you see? I was so angry at you that I denied her the help she needed."

I didn't know what to say. We stood for long minutes,

Jen not looking at me, whispering *I'm so sorry* over and over. Whether to me, to herself or to the baby, I didn't know.

The girl still hadn't moved. I felt the strangest urge: I wanted to rush in and hold her tight, as if I could protect her from all the misfiring DNA in her cells. But she was isolated, I could see, my touch too dangerous for her.

"What... what is she called?"

She couldn't get the name out at first. Then more tears came and she sobbed it out.

"Purity," she said. "I called her Purity."

We parted back at the jump node. Fury at what she had done was burning away my numbness now. But she looked suddenly so small standing by the entranceway, drained by the effort of confession. What had she been through in the past year? She tried to meet my gaze. I wanted to say something to her but couldn't find the words.

※

I did nothing for three days except sleep and eat. I still had to find Ringo but couldn't even get out of bed. The headaches were getting worse. I dreamed about Jen and Purity. Especially Purity, condemned to such a small life. When I woke, I lay in my bed and stared up at the familiar cracks in my ceiling and thought about her. And, for some reason, about John, Paul, George and Ringo. I'd always thought of them as grown men. But before that they would have been children, and before that babies. And what I found myself deciding was not to complete the Cross job after all. Half the DNA was no good to them. I would be in the clear.

But another voice said, *think of the money*. Once I had the Cross's riches I could do anything. Make amends if I wanted.

The thoughts chased each other round my head and I lay there a helpless spectator. In the end, just to break the cycle, I contacted the two Ringo dealers again. One wanted to trade immediately.

We set up a netmeet on neutral ground. His virtual presence, when he arrived, was shadowy and featureless, but the encryption was obviously shoddy. I knew I was behaving like an amateur, playing with amateurs. I could almost hear Devi chuckling at me. But I just wanted to get the case over.

"You have the code?" I asked.

"You have the money?"

It was the classic dilemma of illicit deals throughout history. Who would hand over first? I was in no mood for games.

"I'll give you 25%." I said. "If the DNA checks out I give you the rest."

"50%."

The price was laughable, far more than I'd paid for John or George. But Paul had cost me nothing and it wasn't my money anyway. It suddenly didn't seem that important; it was just numbers. I sent him half the agreed price. After a few moments the DNA image came over and I ran it through my sim plugin.

I knew immediately it was junk; the routines bombed out on load.

"Send me the money back and we'll say no more. This is worthless."

"We had a deal. You think you can fuck with me?"

"Look, keep 5% for expenses," I said. "Give me the rest and we'll go our separate ways."

"I want my money."

But I had already cut the connection. I was instantly back in my bed in my trashed stackroom, the ceiling and its cracks still there above me.

Almost immediately I was contacted again. The other Ringo supplier. Or, more likely, the same guy. Trying to play me.

"Yeah?" I said in as bored a voice as possible.

"Are you still interested in Ringo Starr?"

Pretending he didn't know anything. Driving up the value by restricting the supply.

"Only if I can test first."

We haggled for a time. He offered to send me a 95% complete image if I paid 50% first. I refused to go above 25%. He tried wheedling, then threats. I ignored both. In the end he caved in.

This time, the image checked out nicely against the historical Ringo. I sent another 50% of the money. He sent the remaining 5% of the DNA. Again, it matched. Instead of the remaining 25% I thanked him with exaggerated politeness and killed the connection. It made me feel a little better.

I lay back on my bed, head throbbing inside and out. But I had it. A complete Fab Four genome. I could hand it over in twenty-four hours and be done. I ordered up some Chinese food, wolfed it down, then slept for twelve hours straight.

※

The following day I pinged Devi to send him his money. He'd sweated long enough. Plus I wanted to gloat. But the AI at the hospital switched from businesslike to sympathetic in an instant when I said who I wanted.

"Are you a friend?"

"I visited last week." I released my ID.

"Mr. Simms, I have to inform you that Devindra Singh died two days ago. There were complications arising from his regeneration procedures."

Shock jolted through me. Devi's treatment was routine. I closed the connection. It was several minutes before it occurred to me I was an even richer man now.

For half an hour I paced my room, deciding what to do. I contacted the church in Liverpool. This time it was a human that answered but her tone was similar. A jump fault had scrambled Jones one week before. Such blips were the stuff of urban legend, the set-up for countless dramas and comedies. But in practice they never happened. I tried Ramon. The address didn't even pick-up.

With alarm pounding through me I contacted the Refuge. Jen wasn't there. I asked about the McCartney clone but of course they wouldn't discuss it. I tried Jen directly but the ping went nowhere.

This time I ran to the jump node in ten minutes, no overlays, my mind cold fury.

)0(

They were clearly expecting me. James and Maya Cross stood waiting, a semi-circle of expressionless guards behind them.

"You have the rest of the genome?" asked James.

"I do," I said, trying to sound businesslike. "Safely encrypted in my brain."

"Is this some poor attempt at negotiating a higher fee?" asked James.

"I need to know what you've done with Jen."

"Who is Jen?"

"You know exactly who she is," I said, my cool demeanour wavering. "What have you done with her? Is she dead?"

"As it happens, she's alive," said Maya, speaking for the first time.

"Where?"

"Why would we tell you that?"

My heart was thumping and the pain in my head was hammering along with it. I could see no alternative.

"You might want to watch this."

I began to stream video across to their plugins. James smiled. I had the clear impression events were proceeding as he thought they might. I ignored him and monitored what I was sending.

214

There were the three of us watching the concert, James listening while I gave him the legalities. The bored look on his face was just as I remembered it. The words of his reply were very clear. *We both know the law is irrelevant. But we can pretend if it makes you feel better.*

"I have the whole conversation," I said. "It may not be enough to convict but it would clearly be damaging. Let me have Jen and I'll keep it to myself."

There was a pause while they conversed. I tried to breathe deeply. These were dangerous waters.

"Well," said James, "Before we do that, you might like to see our pictures."

Video streamed back into my brain. It was the same scene, taken from a different angle. I sat next to Cross, my foot actually tapping along to the music. I looked tired, my eyelids drooping.

"All that talking wore you out," said James.

A song ended, *Golden Slumbers*, and my head lolled to one side, my eyes shut. I had no memory of this. Anxiety was sharp inside me. This wasn't on the pictures recorded by my own plugin either. How was that even possible? James made a motion towards some of his men and Maya stood up, looking at me for the first time. She crossed out of the shot. Two of the guards picked me up and followed her.

The scene changed to a smaller room with no windows. I was lying on the floor with Maya standing over me. A single bright light shone from behind her. As soon as I saw it, the halo of her hair around her shadowed face, the memories came back like a physical blow. As intended, no doubt.

✕

I woke to see her standing there, her expression invisible. I stood up on rubber legs.

She addressed me. I felt the contact like something

sharp striking my brain. Trying to make sense of what it was experiencing, my mind constructed an image of red laser beams lancing through my eye sockets, passing effortlessly through my defences.

Now I saw another room: a room in my own mind. I looked on as if through a window. Maya stood inside, not moving. The room was partly my stackroom, partly my childhood bedroom. The shelves were covered with familiar objects. The picture of Jen. A toy rocket I had played with and played with as a child. My father's black hat.

Beside Maya stood some sort of animal, a muscular canine with spikes and spines protruding at every angle.

Gently, her fingertips let go of the creature's leash. It began to smash into furniture, sending shelves crashing to the ground. It ploughed into a wardrobe, reducing it to splinters and tattered threads of clothes. I experienced each impact as pain. The creature grew bigger, as if it was consuming, moving faster all the time. The floor was soon carpeted with broken glass and scraps of plastic. Nausea flooded through me. My mind was being smashed to pieces from inside. When all the furniture was destroyed the creature started to charge the walls of the room, making them shake, threatening to knock them down altogether.

Outside, back in the real world, I felt myself slump to the floor, the stone suddenly cold against my cheek. Delusions assaulted my senses: voices shouting, gulfs of blackness opening up around me. I curled up in a ball.

Then Maya spoke in a clear, soft voice that I immediately clung onto, grateful for any salvation.

"I call it Black Dog. It is currently devouring your higher brain functions and will soon have destroyed everything but the little you need to keep your body alive. It leaves you broken but aware, in your lucid moments, of what has happened to you.

XOX

"The good news is, it takes a backup of what it devours. I can reverse the damage. Although your neural map will be encrypted. It will work fine while you have an up-to-date key. Do you understand? The lease lasts for seven days then your brain becomes mush. A fresh key every week and you're fine. Although you might get a few headaches. Now, whatever it is we are currently discussing with you, are you going to start being reasonable?"

I had a sickening image of her walking about the ruins of the room, casually kicking over the remains of walls. It was impossible to think clearly but the basic instinct to survive burned very brightly. Whatever they wanted.

I managed a nod, eyes tight-shut, teeth clenched hard, cutting into my tongue.

Then, in a moment, it was over. The terrible pain went, as if a spiked fist grasping my brain had let go, and I was back to being myself again, out of breath, lying shaking on the floor before her.

"Excellent," she said.

XOX

The pictures stopped. Maya and James Cross wore the same sunny expressions. My head throbbed with the clashing heat, making it difficult to think.

"Have the sequences," I said. "OK. But I want Jen."

They looked at each other for a moment, each wearing the vacant gaze you often saw when people communicated brain-to-brain.

"Well, well, how romantic," said Maya. "OK, Mr. Simms. You have my word."

"But I don't trust you, of course. And if my brain is scrambled the DNA goes with it."

"We have other Genehunters," said Maya. "You only have one brain. And I never lie. You should know that by now."

They were right, of course. I was in no position to argue. I stalled for a moment, searching for an angle, a hold over them. But I could think of nothing coherent.

I sighed and sent across the remaining DNA.

"Good," said Maya. "Now follow me."

She lead me up to the veranda. We strode past the boy, sitting alone on a wall, watching us with sullen eyes. We went into a large, airy room, one wall a single window overlooking the gardens and the ocean beyond. The air was thick with the sickly smell of flowers. She stopped on a circular mosaic which depicted, in countless green and white squares and triangles, an apple cut in half. I stopped next to her, unsteady on my legs, unsure what was happening. It was only when the room disappeared that I understood the mosaic was another jump node.

We were in a vast, factory-like space, the walls grey and windowless. I thought at first it must be their zoo, but there was no one else there. The entire space was filled with couches: banks of four, laid out head-to-head in a cross pattern. There must have been hundreds of them, thousands maybe. A hospital? A ship? I could make no sense of it. At the far end of the room we reached a collection of perhaps fifty individual couches laid out in straight rows.

"Lie here," said Maya. "This machine will decrypt your neural matrix."

I hesitated.

"Better hurry, Mr. Simms."

I lay down. Unfocused doubts teased me, just out of reach. None of this felt right.

"Jen?" I asked.

"Soon," said Maya. "Trust me."

Her face hovered over me for a moment, finally smiling.

Such was my last view of the world. It wasn't what I would have chosen. I felt ice in my veins, a numbing fog overwhelmed me and I saw no more.

※

I felt the sprinkle of summer rain on my face. I opened my eyes, knowing what I would see. The familiar bench with the same Elvis graffiti. The trees with their leaves flickering like shoals of fish. It was warm. The air tasted of smoke. There was no one else in sight. Distantly I could hear trams clanking and sirens blaring from the docks. Liverpool in 1957 looked as it always did.

Three miles east of me, the story was beginning again. Paul and John were meeting for the first time. What would my part be this time? Last time I'd been a mere bystander. Events had run on to 1968 before stopping abruptly. I remembered sitting alone in a pub, freezing weather outside, when the world ended. Other times I'd been closer to them, friends with them. A father-figure even. Or I was just the crazy guy with the wild ideas they wrote into a song. I knew what I was: a small random variation, a bit-part player in the story.

I stood up. I could feel my age as I moved, a deep-seated fatigue in my bones. In this world I was still young, but even the Crosses couldn't stop my real body ageing. How many years had I lain on that couch? I had lost count of the reincarnations. I supposed I should have been thankful to them for these afterlives. As ever, I wondered if this would be the last one. Perhaps my punishment would finally be complete. My use exhausted.

I walked out of Princes Park towards the city centre. Still everything was familiar. The three boys playing football in the street, their goal a painted rectangle on the side of a house. The blackbird sitting on the red-brick wall, tailed cocked, beady eye watching me. I had no way of knowing, of course, whether the simulation was realistic. But it was the only world I knew now.

I walked to the cathedral: the Anglican one, still

incomplete, its stone walls unworn. A few people were dotted around in the great space, silently praying. I could have told them it was all pointless. Only I knew the true nature of God.

I sat, closed my eyes and addressed myself to the Crosses. I had no way of knowing if they were listening. Still, I did what I always did. Asked for forgiveness. For release. I suppose I was really no different from anyone else there. In any case, no one replied.

I prayed until I heard the soft squeaks of her footsteps coming down the aisle towards me. I looked up into Jen's face. She was as beautiful as ever. All our long history together was there in her eyes. Events that had once inspired John and Paul to write a song about us. The thought always made me smile. Out there in the real world, perhaps millions of people now sang it, our song harvested with all the others from these illusory worlds. Our lives immortalised.

She sat down beside me and rested her head on my shoulder. We said nothing. This early on it had all been said. A choir sang from somewhere, their soaring voices seeming to hold up the vaulting roof of the cathedral.

We waited together, preparing to play our bit-parts one more time.

SIMMS' WORLD

Characters and organizations within the Genehunter universe.

Characters

Simms
A genehunter; makes a living tracking down the DNA code of famous individuals for private collectors.

Kelly
A woman Simms used to have a thing with. In Simms' head it's all still going on...

Devi
A genehunter. Sometime partner of Simms. Sometime enemy. And sometimes both.

Sanchez
Another genehunter, one who sadly got killed a while back. It happens.

Fuchs
Another genehunter, way back.

Eckhart
A genehunter who specialises in the dark arts: the dictators and war-criminals of history.

Ballard
A GMAn (an agent of the Genetic Monitoring Agency), responsible for ensuring people like Simms obey the law. Which they don't.

Gideon Jones
A representative of Forty Days, a religious cult that employs Simms for some very special work.

Nemesis
A clONE death squad leader.

Dr. Grendel
A twenty-first century scientist, creator of the cloning vat technology. And, by all accounts, not a nice person.

Jane Douglas
Dr. Grendel's granddaughter.

Raul Cahn
The Director of MegaMeta Corporation.

Mac
Runs the Double Helix bar in San Francisco.

Mann
A client. Employs Simms to track down some DNA for their collection on behalf of Mann's employer.

Tom Jacks
A dead rock star from, like, way back in the twentieth century.

Stella Stiletto
Another dead rock star, bass player with the Zombies of Death.

Organizations and Institutions

The GMA
The Genetic Monitoring Agency; the arm of government responsible for enforcing the cloning and genetic material laws. An agent of the GMA is commonly referred to as a "GMAn". Agent Ballard is one such agent, responsible for keeping tabs on Simms. Among other things...

clONE
An organization dedicated to defending the rights of cloned individuals. If doing so involves shooting, they're calm about it. They really hate genehunters.

Forty Days
A fundamentalist Christian organization that employs Simms to track down some DNA. Which makes no damn sense at all.

The MegaMeta Corporation
A large, powerful multinational. Among many other things they control a large part of the jump network infrastructure.

The Double Helix
If the genehunters have a spiritual home, the Double Helix bar in San Francisco is it. By common consent, neutral territory, where hunters can meet to trade contacts and code in safety.

Eccentric Orbits

Science Fiction short stories 1999-2011

An astronaut alone in the void of deep space. An alien starship capable of destroying all creation. A DNA Detective in search of the genetic code of The Beatles. A terrorist explosion trapped inside a bubble of space/time. A new life-form found in the quantum echoes of the void.

Eccentric Orbits contains seventeen science fiction stories originally published between 1999 and 2011 and now collected together for the first time. Stories range from the very short up to novella length.

"absolutely fantastic ... just incredible"

"These tales will linger in your mind long after you've turned off your Kindle for the night"

Other Worlds

A constellation of wondrous stars...

Other Worlds collects together fifty-two science fiction and fantasy stories that graced the pages of some of the planet's finest speculative fiction magazines and anthologies between 2012 and 2018.

Starships and sorcerers, aliens and demons, space exploration and forbidden magics throng these pages, in stories that are thrilling, amusing, thought-provoking, terrifying and delightful.

Other worlds await...

ABOUT THE AUTHOR

Simon Kewin was born on the misty Isle of Man but now lives deep in the English countryside. He writes fantasy, science fiction and some things that can't make their minds up. He is the author of over 100 published short stories as well as a growing number of novels.

To find out about his other books or just to say hi, hunt him down at:

www.simonkewin.co.uk

Sign up for his newsletter and you'll be the first to know when he has new books out. There are some fine sci/fi and fantasy books to download for free as thanks.